SIFTING EMORY

S. D. GRICE

Dove
Publishers

Bladensburg, MD

Nancy!
God Bless,
Sabu
Eph 6:10-18

SIFTING EMORY

Published by
Inscript Books
a division of Dove Christian Publishers
P.O. Box 611
Bladensburg, MD 20710-0611
www.dovechristianpublishers.com

Scripture quotations, unless otherwise marked, are from THE HOLY BIBLE, NEW INTERNATIONAL VERSION®, NIV® Copyright © 1973, 1978, 1984, 2011 by Biblica, Inc.® Used by permission. All rights reserved worldwide.

ISBN: 978-1-7359529-7-0

Printed in the United States of America

In memory of Mom. I thank my Lord and Savior that in heaven, He has restored one-hundred-fold what dementia took from her.

Author's Note

A good author will write from the heart, and so this book has been birthed by a heart that longs for the world to know Christ and, in so doing, know the Truth. God's heart and mine ache for those revisiting the Old Testament way of life as each is living "as they see fit." All of our sexual struggles are spiritual struggles. God set a clear standard for the proper and only expression of His gift of sex to us. When two people, man and woman, consummate their marriage, they delight our Lord. Any engagement of sex outside His standard is sin that separates us from God, no matter how much love is felt by the heart.

Every day, this spiritual battle is waged in tens of thousands of lives around the world. What is at stake is our very identity and how each individual will spend their eternity. God has written His law, his original intent, in every heart. Sadly, our inherited sin nature blinds many and leads us away from His desire.

This book is for every person embroiled in the struggle of same-sex attractions and gender confusion. It is for the Christian, who wrongly believes they can continue to be in God's will while pursuing a relationship with their same-sex partner. It is for the lost soul practicing homosexuality and not knowing Jesus. It is for every believer who knows a friend or relative or neighbor struggling or embracing homosexuality. It is for parents who have either done everything right or everything wrong or a little of both. And it is for those who would cast stones, or at the other extreme, celebrate with open pride a life that is far away from the Creator. My prayer is that we will begin to see each other through the lens of Christ and leave judgments to the only true Judge. And my greater prayer is that the Holy Spirit will do what no human being can do; that is to convict us all to make Jesus the true Lord of our lives.

Only the Holy Spirit can supply the transforming power to make us new creations. Only He can teach us our identity in Christ and that Jesus has imputed His righteousness to all who believe in Him. No one can work or will themselves out of the strongholds of sin, especially a sin that so completely envelopes the mind, heart, and soul. Only the blood of Jesus can set us free, and oh how much He wants to do just that!

It is not a question of whether one can be gay and Christian. The question is, who will we serve, self or God? It is not a question of having the willpower to change. The question is, will we be completely surrendered to God? It is not a question of love or truth; it is a recognition that love and truth are so entwined, it must always be both. Jesus said He is the way, the truth, and the life, and God said He is love. To approach any spiritual battle with a deficit of either is to hand the enemy a victory, at the expense of not only ourselves but others as well.

Shame, guilt, fear, lies, distortions, overwhelming desires, rationalizations, delusions, and twisted interpretations of God's Word are all tools of Satan himself. Each is designed to be used with a little truth for flavor and a lot of kind, loving, and good feelings to steal, to kill, and to destroy the desires of God for us. Jesus has won the victory for us, but tragically, many will never know and live in His victory.

I pray that in this battle, the struggler will know truth and love as a person. I hope this book will help everyone understand the depth of this struggle and equip the reader to overcome this bondage (for themselves or someone they know). This is a discipleship book, unique but well overdue. May God be with you, and may we all draw near to Him and give Him all praise and honor and glory.

Prologue

"Emory, it's good to see you. How are you?"

"I'm so happy, Aaron, happier than I ever thought possible. I've been thinking about all the years I spent believing and living a terrible lie. You have walked with me through all the shame and guilt and confusion. And more than that, you have helped me understand that even those years have not been wasted. It took a while, but now I know that God uses everything, even our darkest moments, to draw us closer to Him."

Those were the first words Emory Grace Johnson spoke to me at the beginning of our last session together. We had spent a little more than two years in counseling, and neither of us will ever be the same because of it. Emory and her family are incredible examples of the transforming and healing power of the Holy Spirit. I will never forget those sessions with her and the words of godly wisdom she spoke to me that day.

Her father, Lee, and I had been friends for many years. His call for help was admittedly a surprise. But nothing surprises God, and his amazing grace came to life with every part of the Johnson family's testimony, especially for Emory.

You and I seldom know the impact we have on the lives of others. I am one of the blessed few to have received such a revelation. When God brought Emory to my office, I soon learned how he used me to change her life forever.

This is not my story; it is God's story written into Emory's life. My name is Aaron Knox. I'm a Christian counselor, and Emory was one of my very special clients. "Client" is far too sterile a word for our relationship. She is more like a daughter to me. As I got to know her, my life was changed by her courage and determined commitment to God. Many Christians, including me, are prone to be nominal in our beliefs and superficial in our sacrifice. Emory showed me what it really means to take up our cross and follow Jesus. I watched her lay aside her desires, her wants, her feelings, her job, and many of her close relationships in order to obey God. It was not without struggle; in fact, it is a lifelong struggle. But that, my friends, is what it means not only to have Jesus as your Savior but also the Lord of your life.

Some will try to discredit her story. Some will try to twist it. Some will simply ignore the truth of God's ability to transform lives, but God is the deliverer of the impossible and the answer to the inexplicable. He will never stop fighting for us. Emory's life is evidence of everything that he is and everything he can do if we allow him.

So how did we get to this day? How was Emory transformed into the godly woman she now is? To answer that, you need to know the whole story and the spiritual battle that got us all here. Make no mistake. All of the struggles she faced are spiritual battles, but the victory is hers through Christ Jesus.

Chapter 1
Kids & Cookies

1965

$\mathcal{L}$ee pulled his aged truck into the carport and made sure he turned off the lights before he got out. The previous night he had forgotten to turn them off, inviting a dead battery in the morning. He had been uncharacteristically late to work because of the oversight, and that bothered him more than it should have.

Worse still, his tardiness had made him late getting home to his family. Even on the best of days, it seemed he always was pressed for time to do his best at work, spend quality time with Josie and Eva, and fulfill his commitments at the church.

He sighed deeply to fight the impending grumpiness that was edging perilously closer to the surface. "Lord, as hard as this day has been, thank you for my job and my family. I know Josie, especially right now, needs my understating and patience, and I am sure her day was probably a lot rougher than mine."

Walking toward the house, Lee tripped over one of Eva's toys and tumbled to the ground. Landing squarely on his shoulder, he rolled over and felt the pain immediately. Struggling to his side, he looked down and saw the rip in his pants and the drops of blood on his shirt. He felt a stream of blood sliding down his face. Rubbing his forehead, he found the source of all the blood. The cut must have been deep, judging by the growing red stain saturating his clothes.

"Josie!" The aggravation escalated.

The front door opened, and Josie stood above him looking at the scene in horror. She put four-year-old Eva down and closed the door so her daughter did not have to see her bleeding daddy. Josie maneuvered her large frame down the steps and knelt beside Lee.

"Oh my goodness, Lee, are you all right? Oh no, did Eva leave her toys out again? I am so sorry. It's my fault. I should have made sure her toys were put away. I knew you would probably be late getting home tonight, and it would be getting dark."

"Josie, I'm okay, but you have to do a better job teaching Eva to put her toys away. Look, these pants and shirt are both ruined because of carelessness."

"I said I was sorry," Josie pouted.

"I'm sorry, too, Josie. It's been a tough day, and all I wanted to do is get home to you two." Lee reached up and placed his hand on Josie's protruding stomach. "Or should I say you three? How is my baby boy doing in there today?"

Josie breathed deeply. "Emmitt is just fine. He has been a little rowdy this afternoon. I think he wants to come into this world and meet his daddy. My instinct tells me he is going to be just like you."

Lee looked into Josie's eyes and wondered for the millionth time how he had been so lucky to marry his perfect woman. All the day's troubles and inconveniences disappeared when he was with her. He laughed softly and held her close. "Josie, I love you so much. Eva and Emmitt will have the best mommy in all the world."

The front door opened again. Two small eyes peered at them, then grew large.

"Mommy, what have you done? Why did you hurt Daddy? Lookie, Mommy, his face is leaking and dripping on his shirt, and you tore his pants. Daddy, have you been bad?"

Lee and Josie exchanged glances and erupted in laughter. "I'll take this one, Josie. Eva, baby, Mommy did not do this. She is trying to help Daddy after he fell. I'm okay, honey. I am not really hurt. I just need to get cleaned up a little. I'll be good as new in no time. Do you think you and Mommy could help me get up?"

"Sure, Daddy. Come on, Mommy, Daddy needs our help."

"Okay, Eva. Let's do it!"

Together they got Lee to his feet. When he winced at Josie's touch, she gave him a long, concerned look.

"Just a little tender, hon; I'll be fine."

The smell of Josie's chicken pot pie changed his focus completely. "Say, I know what I am smelling—my favorite! Do we get fresh-baked biscuits with it, too? I'm starving and didn't even know it until just now."

"Oh, Lee, you give merit to that old adage about getting to a man through his stomach. Before you get one bite, though, you need to get out of those clothes and take a shower. I think that cut will be okay with some Mercurochrome and a band-aid. Does it hurt much?"

"No, but this shoulder took the brunt of it. I think a shower will help loosen it up. I know the shirt is ruined. What about these pants?"

"Well, I think I can patch them. You can still wear them around the house. We can salvage them for that at least—and for those future sandlot football games with Emmitt."

"You know just what to say to make a man proud. I'm headed for the shower. I'll be back in a flash. You just be sure those biscuits are still warm." He winked and walked a couple of feet toward the bathroom when the phone rang.

"What now?" he stammered.

"You just go on. I'll get it. Scoot now."

Josie walked to the wall phone and picked up the receiver. "Hello, this is Josie."

Eva followed her mom into the kitchen and began playing with the phone cord.

"I see, well I didn't realize the deacons' meeting was tonight. Lee has had a really tough day today. I am sure he forgot about it. Since it is already after six, I'm afraid he will likely be late. But since this is an important meeting about the future of our new Teen Center, I'm sure he will want to be there. I'll tell him as soon as he gets out of the shower. Okay, Mr. Jones, goodbye."

Josie turned to get the biscuits out of the oven and almost fell over Eva. "Eva Jane Johnson! Can you please not get under my feet every time I get on the phone. How many times do I have to tell you the phone cord is not one of your toys? Now go sit at the table until I can get your dinner ready."

She knew as the words came out of her mouth that her tone was far too harsh. She would like to have blamed it on the natural irritability of pregnancy, but that was no excuse. That still voice in her heart whispered convictions she could not ignore. She looked at Eva and saw the tears brimming in her eyes and knew she had hurt her fragile young heart. Walking over to her daughter, she knelt beside her.

"Eva, you know Mommy loves you, don't you?"

"I guess so. I don't mean to be in your way, Mommy."

"Sweetheart, Mommy should not have been so harsh in how I spoke to you. When I ask you to do things, you need to obey me. But I should never make you feel like I am angry at you or that I don't love you. You are my special girl, and I have a great idea. How about if you and I bake some cookies together later? Would you like that, sweetheart?"

"Oh, Mommy, yes."

"What's this about cookies? Are my two favorite girls planning something yummy for tonight's snack time?" Lee walked in, a bandage on his head, fresh clothes, and a big smile.

"Yes, we are. Hey, you clean up pretty well, but I'm afraid we will have to have dinner without you. I'm making you a to-go box. Mr. Jones called to remind you of the deacons' meeting tonight. Apparently, they have some pretty important items to discuss, and he wanted to make sure you were there. I told him you would probably be a little late, but you would be there."

Lee ran his fingers through his damp hair. "How could I forget the deacons' meeting? This is one of the most important meetings we will have this year. You remember I had proposed we start a new mission to reach out to the unchurched teens in our community. This town does not have a single outreach to help those kids. I think Calvary Community

Church should step up and help. Yes, I have to be there. I'm really sorry."

"We understand, Lee. That's why we are planning a big baking party tonight. Bet we have more fun than you do! Since I am eating for two and Eva loves chocolate chip cookies, just know that it will be quite a sacrifice to save some for you, but we will try our best!"

Lee laughed, his good-natured banter taking over, "So that's how it's going to be, huh? Guess I'll just have to convince the deacons as soon as possible about the outreach and get back here pronto."

"Don't worry, Daddy. We always make bunches and bunches. We will save you some, I promise."

Lee kissed his girls, grabbed his dinner, and headed for the door. Looking over his shoulder, he winked and said, "And we are promise keepers in this family."

Chapter 2
Critical Needs

*L*ee woke early the next morning and slipped quietly out of bed. He gazed at his wife and felt bad that he had not gotten home early enough to talk with her. She was a real trooper and his best friend. He could have used a good talk after the disappointing meeting.

He stepped into the bathroom to get ready for work. Laden with so many concerns, he could see the stress on his 30-year-old face. Was that premature gray peeking out from his coal-black hair?

Josie stirred in bed, and he looked into the bedroom to see her deep emerald eyes looking sleepily at him. Her ruby red hair lay in a tangled mess. Not a hint of make-up lined her face. Her crumpled nightgown was stretched to its full limit by her bulging belly. Even now, just as she was, she was the most beautiful woman he had ever seen.

"Hey, Lee. Sorry I couldn't stay up and wait for you last night. Carrying around this extra thirty pounds just wears me down, I guess. What time did you finally get home? How did the meeting go?"

Lee walked over to the bed and sat next to her. He brushed a loose strand of hair from her eyes. Without thinking, he rubbed her belly tenderly and kissed her cheek.

"Josie, it's okay; I'm glad you went to bed. It was

pretty late when I got back. And I thank you and Eva very much for the delicious treat I found waiting for me. It came at the perfect time. I needed some comfort food."

"Oh no, sounds like the meeting didn't go well. What happened?"

"Well, Josie, it's just so hard to convince people to do new things, especially when church funds are in play. The only other guy on board with me was Jim Connors. He knows from personal tragedy what these kids are facing and how much help they need. The other ten deacons, great and good men that they are, fear all kinds of things. I felt pretty defeated when I came home last night. I finally got them to agree to at least let the church body vote on it, so I need to put together a pretty strong proposal by next business meeting."

"Lee, you know I will help you all that I can. I'll bring it up in my Sunday school class, and I'm going to try to teach a few more Bible studies before little Emmitt gets here. I will tell those ladies about it too."

Josie grew silent and serious, "Lee, do you ever worry about bringing up our kids in this world? It seems like the devil has just taken over right now. There is hatred and violence over the color of a person's skin. Our youth seem so sucked into drugs and sex, and the music they listen to fills their minds with all the evils known to man."

Lee put his arms around his trembling wife and hugged her tenderly. He could feel her tears fall on his shoulder. "It's okay, Josie. Our kids are going to be brought up to know and love the Lord. His angels will guard and protect them. But you're right; so many in this world need to know Jesus. We have a chance to do that if we can just convince our church to be burdened for these lost kids as if they were our own."

He continued, "Listen, Josie, I know that what we read in the news and see on television paints a scary picture for the future of our kids. Our world seems to be growing further away from our Creator every day. But never forget that our God is sovereign and all-powerful, and nothing can defeat Him. He loves and cares for his own deeply, and He will never stop fighting for us."

Josie pressed closer to Lee and sighed, "Honey, listening to you always calms me. I think you would make a great pastor. You have such a heart for people."

Lee stroked Josie's hair and smiled, "You must have been talking to Jim. He said the same thing about a career change last night, but I think being an active deacon is where I belong right now. I have a great job, and I have to provide for my growing family."

"But you would be open to it if that were God's will?"

"Josie, it would be a tremendous sacrifice, not only for me but for you and the kids. Finances would be really tight, and the life of a pastor is not easy for him or his family." He took a breath and continued, "But if the Lord made it clear that's where he wanted me, I'd have to say yes."

"I know you would, Lee, and I would do whatever it takes to support you."

"Well, we will cross that bridge if and when it ever comes in sight."

Gathering herself, Josie leaned forward and looked at Lee. "Sorry I get so emotional, but you always know exactly what to say."

"Come on, Josie. Let's go get our little one and have some breakfast."

Josie squeezed Lee's hand tightly. "Okay, would you mind getting Eva? I'll be down soon."

"Sure, hon, I'll even make pancakes. I have time before work. Blueberry sound good?"

"With pickles?" Josie added.

"Huh?'

"You know how we pregnant ladies are, but I'm kidding."

Lee walked down the hall and helped Eva get dressed. Then together, father and daughter, made their way to the kitchen. Lee prepared for his special pancakes while Eva sat at the table looking through her coloring book and humming, "Jesus Loves Me."

"Leeeee! Lee! Come quickly. I need you. Hurry!"

Josie's screams made them both jump. Lee dropped the pan of batter into the sink and raced upstairs, "I'm coming, Josie."

He rounded the corner and saw Josie leaning on the bed post, ghost white. The unmistakable puddle of water at her feet startled him.

"Lee, my water broke. Emmitt is coming. We have to get to the hospital now. Something is not right."

"Your water.....Emmitt....but it's not time. How, why.... where's the bag? Wait, what's not right?" Lee stammered.

"Lee, the pain." She tried to breathe deeply, then collapsed on the bed.

"Josie!" He shook her to bring her back to consciousness, but she was unresponsive. "No, Josie, please God, let her and the baby be okay. Please, God, help us."

Chapter 3
The Unexpected Blessing

*L*ee paced anxiously across the linoleum tiles at Grace Memorial Hospital. He glanced again at his watch. He had been there more than two hours with no updates. His mind was racing, and everything was a blur. He vaguely remembered getting Eva to the neighbors' house. Then the ambulance came, and the medic said something about blood pressure and pregnancy complications. *What was going on? Everything was fine, and then it wasn't. The baby was not due for another three weeks. Was Josie going to be okay? What about the baby?*

He looked down at his shaking hand and then realized his whole body was trembling. He had never known such fear and utter helplessness. He felt a tap on his shoulder and expectantly whirled around, coming eye to eye with Pastor Timothy. Lee broke. Tears poured from his eyes. Pastor Timothy held him as he sobbed uncontrollably, neither speaking a word.

"Excuse me, are you Mr. Johnson?" A short, plump doctor in blue scrubs peered over his glasses at Lee and Timothy.

"Yes, yes, I am. How is my wife? And the baby, is he okay? Please, Doctor, please tell me?"

"Mr. Johnson, I am happy to tell you everything is fine. We were able to quickly stabilize all of your wife's vitals, and after that, everything else went smoothly. We delivered your baby in perfect health just a few minutes ago. There were no complications from the early arrival. They are both fine."

"They are both fine?! Did you hear that, Pastor Tim? They are both fine. Josie and my baby boy are both alive and well. Praise the Lord!"

"Praise the Lord indeed, brother," Pastor Timothy smiled.

"Can I see them? Can I be with them now? I can't wait to tell Josie how much I love her and to hold my baby boy,"

"Uh, about that, Mr. Johnson."

"Lee, just call me Lee. What's wrong? Is there something I should know?"

"Well, first of all, I want to assure you that absolutely nothing is wrong. But there has been a bit of an unexpected development—a surprise, if you will. However, I feel like it is Josie's place to tell you, not mine. Follow me, and I will take you to your family."

Bewildered, Lee fell in step behind the doctor. Fatigue, relief, and gratitude all seemed to squeeze together in his thoughts.

"Congratulations, Lee. I will be sure to pass on to the church all your good news."

"Oh, Pastor, I am so sorry; I didn't mean to walk away from you. I appreciate your prayers more than words can say. Yes, please thank everyone for us. I will be sure and update you on everything as soon as I can."

"Sure, Lee, don't worry about anything. You take care of those precious ones."

When they finally reached Josie's room, Lee pushed open the door quietly but could hardly restrain his excitement. What he saw next was one of the most beautiful sights a man could behold. Josie sat in the bed holding a bundle of newborn life. The white blanket was wrapped securely around his boy, obscuring his view. Lee kissed Josie tenderly.

"Hi, honey, guess this is my baby boy you've got here. He is beautiful—even has your red hair already."

"Hi Lee, we made it," Josie hesitated for a moment and continued, "Lee, I have to tell you something, and I'm not exactly sure how best to do it."

"What is it, Josie?" Lee reeled. "The doctor said something about an unexpected development?"

"Yes, that is what I am trying to tell you. I'm afraid we are going to have to change the baby's name. You see, we cannot name him Emmitt because our boy is a girl!"

"What? How can that be? All the doctors said definitely a boy, and we bought all this baby boy stuff. Goodness, what am I saying? We have a beautiful girl, and I thank God so much for her."

"Not disappointed?"

"Not at all. I love her. Just look at her. God gave us another girl. What a blessing! What about her name? Guess you haven't had much time to think about it."

"Actually, I have. It came to me pretty quickly. You know how we wanted to name the baby after my grandfather, Emmitt Martin, right?

"Right."

"Well, I remember growing up hearing my grand-dad tell us stories about his favorite pastime as a boy in East Tennessee. His gang of friends would go down to the swimming hole and spend the entire day there. Then they would get something to eat and go back in the evening to catch fish out of the same river."

"Okay, Josie, but what does this have to do with the baby's name?"

"Well, I still want to honor Granddad in some way, so how about if we pick the name of his favorite river—the Emory River. What do you think of Emory Grace Johnson?"

"Emory Grace Johnson," Lee pondered. "What a beautiful name for our beautiful girl! I love it, and so will she when we tell her about her namesake."

"Do you want to hold her, Daddy?"

"Oh, do I ever." Lee gingerly took the bundled baby from Josie. Holding her tight against his chest, he looked down at the sleepy eyes and marveled at the miracle in his arms.

"Hey there, sweet girl. I'm your daddy, and I love you so much. I will always be here for you. Don't ever forget that. No matter what, I will always and forever love you. Emory Grace, your mother and I promise to care for you and protect you and, most of all, tell you all about Jesus."

Lee sat down in the nearby rocking chair and sang softly to his precious gift. He looked over at Josie, who had fallen asleep, and thanked God for his family.

Chapter 4
Seeds of Rejection

1970, five years old

*E*ight children, all talking at once, sat around the table. They were there to celebrate Emory's fifth birthday. Josie had wanted to invite all the kids from Emory's Sunday school class, but the house had a limited capacity, and so did the Johnson family budget.

Emory sat at the head of the table, proud to be the guest of honor. Despite all of Josie's efforts to convince her daughter not to wear her favorite baseball shirt and cap, Emory happily sported both.

"Josie, what can I help you with?

"Thank you so much, Karen, for being my third and fourth hand. I think we are about ready for cake and ice cream. All the kids are so cute. I just wish I could have convinced Emory to wear something a little nicer than her ball gear. She is such a tomboy. I bet she could compete with any boy—even boys older than she is."

Karen laughed, "Oh, Josie, let her be a kid. She will grow out of it. For now, just let her enjoy being just who she is."

"I know you are right, of course, Karen, but sometimes I think she instinctively knows all the plans we had made for a boy when she was born and is just playing the part. Sorry, Karen, I am being ridiculous. Now let's see, if you will get the ice cream from the refrigerator, I'll grab the cake, and we will get this party started. The kids are getting rowdy, so we better get them served."

Eva sat next to Emory and laughed at her when Josie put the cake on the table. She taunted her, "Ha, Emory, look at your little bitty cake. Mine was twice as big and twice as good. I told you Mommy and Daddy love me more. I'm their little girl and look at you. You were not supposed to be a girl, too. Why couldn't you just go ahead and be a little boy? You look like one, and you smell like one. You are gross like all boys."

Josie was quick to step in, "Eva Jane Johnson, you stop that right now. You will never say such a thing to Emory again. Those words are mean and hurtful, and I will not have it in this house. Do you understand me?"

"Yes, Mommy," Eva cried.

"Now, I want you to apologize to your sister and then go into the living room until I call you."

"But..."

"No but's, Eva. Go ahead and do what I said."

Eva murmured an insincere apology and walked head down out of the dining room. She glanced back for a moment and made a face at Emory.

"Karen, I just don't know what to do about those two. They are so very different. Eva is a good kid, but she teases Emory mercilessly. And Emory, just look at her, not a tear, not a word. She just takes it all in and withdraws. Honestly, I wish Lee would hurry up and get here. He will make her smile and laugh as if none of this ever happened. When I try to console her, she doesn't even respond to me. It really started getting worse a few months ago when I began taking her to the babysitter's house while I worked at the Teen Center. I've talked to the sitter, and she said at first, all Emory did was cry for about an hour. Now she just sulks a little then perks up with game time. I think she might start believing some of the things Eva says to her."

"Josie, your kids are just at that age, I'm afraid. Kids can be very cruel to each other, especially sisters sometimes. I know I targeted my little sister for a while, but now we are best friends. I really believe it is just plain and simple jealousy. You know Eva was mommy and daddy's little girl for four years. She had you all to herself. Then along came this unexpected girl who is a rival for your attention."

"I know, Karen, and I wish somehow Lee had not gone on and on to Eva about how she was going to get a little brother. We were all so taken off guard when Emory was born, and Eva was so upset. I remember her first words to her sister were, 'What are you doing here? We ordered a boy. Take her back, Mommy.' It was funny and cute then, but she has not grown out of it."

"She will, Josie. She will. I know how much you and Lee love both of your girls. Don't you ever think that you are not a good parent. You are great with kids of all ages. I have seen you work with kids, and you are amazing at the Teen Center."

"The Center is really a good thing for the kids in this community. You know a lot of them are from homes with single moms. Sadly, many of the moms do not work and sit at home all day watching *The Guiding Light* or *Peyton Place*. How it must grieve the

Lord to watch these kids who are never taught a single thing about who he is and how much he loves them."

"I am so grateful to you and Lee for getting the Center finally approved and opened. I know it was an uphill battle to get the church members to approve it, but now that it is open, they can see what a tremendous difference it makes."

"Mommy?"

"Yes, Emory, sweetheart?"

"When is Daddy going to get here? The ice cream is already melting, and he promised he would be here for my party."

"He will be here anytime now, Emory. He wouldn't miss your party for anything in the whole wide world, but we do need to go ahead and light those candles so we can eat cake. All of our guests are getting hungry."

"No, no, no, Mommy, not until Daddy gets here. No cake or ice cream until he gets here. He has to see me blow out my candles."

"But Emory, we are not sure when he will be here, and your friends are hungry. We really have to go ahead and...."

"No, Mommy. Why do you have to be the meanest mommy in the world? Why can't my birthday be as good as Eva's when Daddy was here, and we all laughed? Why do I always have to take second place? Even when Eva does bad things, you always talk to her and never to me."

Stunned, Josie shot an anguished look at Karen. Emory's words broke her mother's heart. Never had Emory made it so clear what her feelings were. In a way, Josie felt some relief that Emory had finally opened up and expressed herself. But that expression was like a blowtorch that incinerated Josie's confidence as a parent. Dispirited and shaken, she opened her mouth to tell Emory how much she was loved and that Eva was not a favored child, but the words would not come out. She had said them hundreds of times before, but it was clear Emory did not believe her. Why? How had she failed to show her youngest girl how much she meant to everyone in the family? The enmity between sisters was one thing, but this chasm between her and Emory was overwhelming. Apparently, Emory only felt loved by her father.

"Hey there, everybody. I'm here. Where is my birthday girl?"

"Daddy!"

Lee scooped Emory up in his arms. It was the first time Emory had actually laughed all day.

"So, I hear from all the television and radio shows that Emory Grace Johnson is having a birthday party here today."

"That's right, and here are all my friends, and here is the ice cream and cake. I made Mommy wait until you got here to watch me blow out my candles like you did with Eva on her birthday."

"Well, good. Looks like I got here just in time. Let's see now; I believe you are, what, eighteen years old today?"

"Daddy, you are so silly. I'm five. See, look, five candles on the cake."

"Daddy?" a voice called from the far corner.

Lee looked to see Eva sheepishly standing in the doorway. "Eva sweetie, what are you doing in there? Come on, let's sing 'Happy Birthday' to your sister and eat some of this great cake your mother baked."

"I helped Mommy bake the cake, Daddy. Emory doesn't like to bake. She would rather be outside all the time."

Josie bit her lip and pushed aside the earlier heart-wrenching episode. Handing the box of matches to Lee, her head and heart throbbed.

"Lee, go ahead and light the candles, please." She just wanted this party to be over, to get all these kids out of her house, and to cry herself to sleep. Worthless as a parent and unable to help her children, what had become of her?

Lee saw Josie's shaking hands as he took the matches. Instinctively, he knew she was in a crisis, and all the kids prevented him from caring for her. He gave her a long, penetrating look and took her hand. Squeezing it lovingly, he mouthed the words, "I love you."

Maybe having her work at the Teen Center was a bad idea. She was so good for the teens, and no one else would step up to be director, but at what cost? She seemed happy to do it, but it had been hard to leave Emory with a sitter. Eva had been fine; she was in school all day anyway and more mature. Emory, though, had taken it hard. Was she angry at Josie? Did she feel abandoned? Surely not. It was only three days a week, and Josie did everything for both of the girls.

Even with the cloud of hurt and bewilderment, Josie continued to put on a brave front for the remainder of the party. Cake was eaten. Games were played. Presents were opened. When Karen left with the last child, Emory went outside; and Eva retreated to her room to play dress up.

22

Josie fell into Lee's arms, sobbing uncontrollably. "Lee, I am such a failure as a mother. My child will not even speak to me. She called me the 'meanest mommy in the world.' Lee, how can she not know how much I love her?"

Lee held Josie for several minutes. He listened to her pour out her hurt to him, knowing it was not answers she needed, but just for him to listen and hold her. Her world had been turned upside down, and he would have to be her steady rock until she regained her equilibrium. Finally, her sobs settled into suffering whimpers, and she pulled back to look at Lee's face.

"Lee, what have I done wrong?"

"Josie, sweetheart, you are a wonderful mother. You have done nothing wrong. Emory loves you more than she can put into words. She is only five, and five-year-olds can say some pretty hurtful things and not even realize it. She is a very sensitive child underneath that tough exterior, and I know how much Eva teases her. We have to remember that her perceptions are sometimes a little different from reality. Don't worry, Josie. Emory knows you love her."

"I hope so, Lee."

"Josie, I know with everything that has been going on today, this is not the best time to bring this up, but it's pretty urgent. You might even say a matter of life and death, really."

Her smile faded, replaced by concern yet again. "What is it, Lee? What is wrong?"

"Take it easy, Josie. Nothing is wrong, but we have a decision to make that cannot be put off. You know the girls have been begging us to get a dog for months.

"Yes, go on."

"I was late getting home because I stopped off at the Humane Society. Honey, I found the most beautiful dog. He is four years old and is a mix but looks like he is mostly a Springer Spaniel. His owner loved him but had to move away and couldn't take him. The dog has been at the shelter for almost six months, but they say his age is inhibiting adoption. Most people want cute puppies. The worst news is that tomorrow will be his last day. If no one takes him, they have no choice but to put him down."

"Lee, you really know how to pull on my heart strings, don't you? We will need to make some ground rules and enforce them, you know."

"I know. I know. This will be a good teaching opportunity for them. Pepper will make a great companion and maybe help Emory get past Eva's taunts."

"Pepper is it, huh? Where did you get that name?"

"The previous owner gave it to him, and once you see him, you'll understand why. He has cute little black speckles on all four of his white paws. Josie, you are going to love him, and so will the girls. What do you say?"

"Well, of course, I say yes even if he is a house dog, which I am pretty sure he is, but you intentionally neglected to tell me that part."

"You know me too well. He is."

"Just don't forget what I said about ground rules, Lee. When issues come up about Pepper, we have to be consistent with the dog and with the girls."

"Absolutely, I am with you."

"When do we get him?"

"I will call tonight. We will get a stay of—well, you know—the other plans they have for him. I will pick him up tomorrow after work."

"Lee, I have to admit I am excited about Pepper. Can't wait to see the girls' reactions. Maybe Emory will even realize that I'm not the meanest mommy in the world."

Chapter 5

Shining Star

1976, 11 years old

"Come on, Pepper. Come on, boy. Let's go play until it gets dark. See you, Mom."

"Remember what I told you, Emory. You two get back in here as soon as the sun goes behind the mountain. Keep Pepper out of the mud this time, please."

"Okay, Mom. Come on, boy."

Pepper raced ahead of Emory as she held the door open. Running out to catch up with him, she let the storm door go. The familiar slam put everyone in the house on notice that Emory and her best friend had left the building.

Josie stood over the sink, shaking her head in mild agitation. "I swear, Lee, that girl and her best buddy have no limit to their energy. I give up on the poor storm door. As long as the two of them live here, it will just have to endure the abuse."

Lee laughed at his wife's mock exasperation. "It's the sweet sound of a happy kid, Josie. There's nothing like it. You wouldn't change it if you could. It is a delight to both of us."

"You're right, Lee. Pepper is her best buddy for sure. It was pretty clear that first night you brought him home six years ago when they both insisted on sleeping in the same bed. I can't believe we let them do it then—and every night since. You know, I really believe that if Pepper were not allowed to sleep in Emory's bed, she would get up and sleep with him wherever he lay down for the night."

"You're probably right. They sure are made for each other. Say, where did Eva go after dinner?"

"I'm not sure, but I do have a pretty good guess. She is doing what all fifteen-year-old girls do. She is either on the phone talking to her friends about what boy likes which girl, or she is in the bathroom experimenting with new ways to fix her hair. Speaking of Eva, it is going to be time really soon to start allowing her a little more freedom. She will be sixteen, and we are already allowing her to do sleepovers with the girls. Daddy's little girl is becoming a beautiful young woman. Boys are taking notice, Lee. Are you?"

Lee sighed, "Josie, where in the world has time gone? My little girl, already almost sixteen? Say it isn't so, please. Seems like yesterday, we were playing on the swings and telling her to quit teasing her sister so much."

"Thank goodness, she grew out of that jealous rivalry she had with Emory! I think Pepper helped a little with that. Once Pepper took to Emory, Eva felt like she had Daddy to herself again. Eva is really a good girl. She loves cooking for me when I am running late, and I hope our mother-daughter girl talks will continue."

Lee shook his head in agreement. "Last year when she accepted Jesus as her Lord and Savior—oh, what a day that was. I think I took thirty pictures of her baptism."

"Ha, more like fifty pictures, but I don't think you

could ever take too many pictures of our child's baptism."

"Josie, what about Emory? Do you think she is becoming aware of what salvation means?"

"I've been thinking about that, Lee. You know lately, she has been asking a lot of questions. She is so amazed by all the natural beauty in the world. She soaks things in at a very deep level. I think her heart is receptive to the Holy Spirit's convictions. I just keep trying to watch and be ready. It could be any time, I believe."

"That is great news. She asks me questions, too, mostly about sports and cars, but in our few serious moments, she asks about Jesus. Seems every night when I listen to her prayers, she has that childlike wonder and belief in our heavenly Father. You know, every night when I tuck her and Pepper in bed, I tell her I love her, and she tells me she loves me, too, and she loves Jesus because he made Pepper."

"Daaad, Daad, I need you. Can you come up here for a minute? My hairdryer is not working."

"Well, there's your answer about Eva's whereabouts. You go ahead and play super Dad to her. I'm going to go out and call Emory and company to come in."

"Got ya'. See you on the couch for *Gunsmoke* and popcorn later?"

"It's a date, you smooth talker. Matt Dillon's got nothing on you."

Josie kissed Lee and went out the door, quietly closing it behind her. She looked down the block in both directions—no sign of the duo.

The sun had made a rapid descent, and the air had chilled precipitously. "Should have brought a jacket." Raising her voice as she walked through the grass, she called, "Emory, Emory, come home. It's dark, and you promised."

In the distance, a dog barked. It was Pepper's distinctive call. Though never really afraid for their safety, Josie still felt a small twinge of relief. They were safe and close by. Just over the ridge near the old Elm tree, she saw Emory's incomparable mop of red hair sneaking out from under her baseball cap. How could she and Emory look so much alike and have so few interests in common?

Emory ran with ease through the pasture, Pepper not far behind. She was so fast that even Pepper had to press hard to maintain the pace. Those young, lanky legs sprang with easy vitality. Josie could only marvel at her youngest daughter's athleticism. No wonder every sports team in the county wanted her.

"Hey, Mom! We made it! We are here. Pepper started chasing a squirrel, so we are just a little bit late, but not much."

"No, not much. You and Pepper are forgiven. But I have a question for you. How on earth can you run that fast for that distance and not be out of breath? I'd be on the ground asking for oxygen.'"

"Oh, Mom, you are so silly. As Dad would tell me, I guess I am just made by God that way."

"You truly are your father's child. Poor Pepper, you are going to run the old boy's legs off. You know, he is ten years old now."

"I know, Mom, that's seventy in dog years, but I keep him in good shape, and he eats good food. Look, I even kept him out of the mud like I promised."

"Well done, Emory. Are you ready to go in now?"

"Almost, Mom, but could we stay out just a little bit

longer to watch the stars come out? One of my most favorite things about living out here in the country is seeing all those millions of twinkling stars."

"I know just what you mean, Emory; God really shows off in the brilliance of all his shining stars, doesn't he? Come on. Let's sit on our trusty bench and watch."

Emory and Pepper followed Josie to the old bench that Josie's father had carved. It had special meaning and memories, especially for Josie, who used to sit there with her own father and count the stars.

"Mom?"

"Yes, honey?"

"God really, really loves us, doesn't he?"

"Oh, yes, Emory, more than we know."

"He even loves us when we are bad and don't deserve his love, doesn't he?"

"Yes, Emory. In fact, God knows absolutely everything about us—even the things we think, and he loves us anyway. Only God can love us so completely."

"Does he love us more than he loves his own son, Jesus?"

"No, not more than Jesus."

"Then why did God send Jesus to die on the cross? God is in charge of everything, so he could have saved Jesus. Instead, he told Jesus to let them kill him so we could be saved."

"Emory, I can tell you have really been paying attention in church and to what your father and I have told you about Jesus. Let me see if I can explain it a little better for you. I know it is a little hard to understand why the all-powerful God would let his son suffer so much, but when Adam and Eve sinned against God, every one of us who has ever been born since then inherited a sin nature. It took the sacrifice of Jesus' life for us to be restored so our sins would not keep us out of heaven."

"Yes, I remember the story of Adam and Eve, and I understand what it means to inherit something—like I inherited your read hair."

"That's right, very good."

"But what does 'sin nature' mean?"

"Good question. Let's start with the word 'sin.' You know what a sin is, don't you?"

"Yes, Mom, it's when we do things that are against what God wants us to do. He tells us what he wants, but we don't do it. It's like we disobey him."

"Good, Emory. That's exactly right. When we sin, we are acting very selfishly, and that comes naturally to us. In other words, we don't learn it; we are born with the desire to do things our own way, not God's way. We want what makes us feel good, and we don't want to share with others. Some people lie or cheat or steal for money. Others become jealous and angry and do hurtful things just so they can win out. There are all kinds of ways that the sin nature can make people do bad things. See, in our sin nature, we are a slave to sin. The more we sin, the more we want to sin and the farther away we get from God. Eventually, if we do not confess our sins and repent, which means to change our ways, we will be controlled by sin. What is really amazing is that if we surrender to God, his Holy Spirit comes and lives inside of us, and sin will never control us again."

"So why does God let people sin? Isn't he in control of everything?"

"Yes, God is always in control no matter what situation you are in. This is a big word, but he is called 'sovereign,' like a king who rules over his kingdom. God rules over everything he has created."

"And he created everything, right?'

"That's right, he is King of kings...."

"And Lord of lords!"

"Correct again. You ask why he allows people to sin when he could stop them. That's a tough question, but he gives every person free will. That is, all of us are free to make up our own mind. Either we decide to follow Jesus and obey him, or we decide we are going to do things our own way and think we can live without God."

"But, Mom, why would anyone want to live without God, to live without love?"

"I believe it is mostly because people really do not understand how evil our sins make us. We have an enemy named Satan who lies and twists everything. Like Eve, we see something we like and take it even when God has said no. In this world we live in, sin is everywhere, and it seems like the only people who get what they want are the biggest of the sinners. So even though God sent his Son to die in our place and he offers us a chance to be with him forever, to believe that requires faith. Faith is believing in the things we cannot see."

"I believe God loves me and sent Jesus to die in my place so I can live forever in heaven, Mom."

"Do you believe that Jesus arose from the grave after he died?'

"Yes, I do, and I believe Jesus is in heaven and will be there to welcome me one day. I am going to ask Him if Pepper can come with me."

Josie's heart raced. Could it be that the Holy Spirit

had convicted Emory and given her saving grace and faith?

"So let me make sure we understand each other, okay?"

"Sure."

"You understand that you are a sinner, that you and I were born that way, and we have done or said things that made God unhappy. You also believe God sent his Son Jesus to take our place and be judged for our sins. Right so far?"

"That's right, and I can tell you more. I believe that if Jesus had not died for my sins, I could never be one of God's kids because all his kids must be as perfect as Jesus. That is all really, really great, but even better, Jesus is not dead. He is alive, and it is sin that is dead. And you know what, Mommy?"

"Tell me what, Emory."

"I've got Jesus living right here in my heart now."

Josie could not contain her joy. She was certain that Emory had really received Jesus as her Lord and Savior. She reached over and pulled her into her arms. "Emory, you surely do, and he always will be there. He promises to never leave you. Come on. Let's go tell your dad, and then on Sunday, you can talk to Pastor Timothy."

Chapter 6
Salvation & Sifting

*E*mory could hardly wait for the Sunday morning service to be over so she could tell everyone in the church about her good news. She looked at her Dad sitting up on the platform as the associate pastor and was so happy he was her daddy.

As she fidgeted in her seat, her Mom put her arm on her leg and gave her the "please sit still or you will be in big trouble" look. Complying immediately, she dutifully settled her outward behavior, but inside, her heart beat faster with each passing minute.

Pastor Timothy finished his closing prayer and gave the invitation, "So today if there is anyone who has been convicted by the Holy Spirit to accept Jesus as Lord and Savior, now is the time come to the alter. He is calling you to victory over sin and death. Come just as you are. Don't worry about anything else. Don't put this decision off for another time. Not a single one of us is guaranteed our next breath in this world, so you come now."

"Now, Mom? Can I go now?'

Josie grabbed Emory's hand gently and smiled. "You bet, Emory; let's go."

As Emory stepped out of the pew and into the aisle, a wave of excitement coursed through her body. It became more of child leading the adult than the more traditional scenario.

Lee stepped down to greet them. Emory looked up and saw him smiling through the tears. "Hi, honey," Lee's voice choked with emotion. "I am so happy for you."

"Hi, Daddy. I want to tell everyone Jesus is in my heart."

Pastor Timothy joined the family, "And, Emory, everyone in this congregation is going to celebrate your announcement. Now you remember everything we talked about this morning before church, don't you?"

"Oh yes, and I am certain that Jesus saved me from my sins."

"And you know it was by his grace through faith that you are saved?"

"Yes, Pastor Tim. I know that it is nothing I did. I could never be good enough to deserve heaven, and because of Jesus, I don't have to be."

"That's right, Emory, so I want you and your family to sit here for a minute and let this lady get some information from you. In a few minutes, we will tell everyone about your amazing decision."

Emory sat with her parents while the church secretary went over things with her dad. Finally, Pastor Timothy raised his hand to end the music.

"I thank you all for being here today, and I have some fantastic news to share with you. Lee, will you and Josie and Emory join me and face the congregation? Most of you know the Johnson family. Their other daughter Eva is on a school trip to the nation's capital this week, but the rest of the family is here today. Emory has made a major decision she wants to share with you."

Pastor Tim looked down at Emory and winked,

"Okay, Emory, shall I tell everyone, or would you like to tell them?"

"Oh, I want to tell them!"

"I thought you might," Pastor Tim laughed. "The floor is all yours, Emory. Here, you can use my microphone."

"Thanks, Pastor Tim. So, everybody, I just want to tell you that I have accepted Jesus as my Savior. And I want to say it is the best thing that I have ever done. If you have not welcomed Jesus into your heart, you need to do it; you really do. It is great! Guess that's all for now. Here's your microphone, Pastor Tim."

An elderly lady rose to her feet and shouted, "Amen and praise the Lord."

Soon the entire congregation stood with her and applauded. Emory laughed and looked at her dad. "Wow, Dad!"

"Emory, my precious child, everything you are seeing here is happening in heaven, too."

"I know, Daddy. I dreamed about the celebration in heaven last night."

"You did?"

"Sure did."

"What did you see?"

"Well, it was like this. All of the angels were together, and the one they called Michael appeared at the foot of the throne of God. Jesus was sitting on the right side of the throne, and he stood up above Michael. He was smiling. His eyes were gentle and kind like yours, Dad.

Lee was stunned but smiled and urged her to continue. "What happened then?"

"Well, then Jesus slowly raised his hand and told the angels to be still." Remembering her mom's earlier impatience with her, Emory looked at her mother. "See, Mom, even angles get fidgety sometimes."

"Yes, Emory, I guess they do. Please, honey, tell us the rest."

"Well, when they all calmed down, it was so quiet. Then the most amazing thing happened. Jesus began to speak. His voice was the most wonderful sound I have ever heard."

Now all three adults were fully engulfed in Emory's retelling of her divine dream. Pastor Tim eagerly asked, "What did Jesus say, Emory? Do you remember?"

"Oh, of course. I remember everything in my dream. He said to the angels, *'You are my faithful ones, for you offer praise in truth to the all-powerful living Lord. Today we celebrate the salvation of Emory Grace Johnson, for she now has passed from death unto life. Michael, the Book of Life, please.'* Then Michael stepped up and opened the Book of Life to a marked page, and I saw my name written in black ink in it."

"Honey, that is amazing that God gave you a peek into heaven to see all of that," Josie exclaimed.

"Wait, Mom, there is more, and this is the best part. Jesus spoke again and said, *'Emory, has chosen today to accept my grace and faith given by the convictions of my Spirit. I have seen into her heart and know that she truly accepts me as her Savior and her Lord.'* All the angels started singing and praising Jesus for his work in my life. Then they lifted their hands celebrating because they said I was now a part of the family of God."

Emory stopped to catch her breath, then continued. "Finally, Jesus continued his speech, *'You are*

my witnesses that Emory's name was written in my Book of Life before the foundation of the world, but today her name is fully sealed. Today she is a new creation; the old is gone, and the new has come. One day, when I call her home and when death takes her from her body, she will forever be with me in heaven.'
Then Michael held the Book level before Him. Jesus touched his nail-scarred left wrist with his right finger. Blood transferred to his finger, and I saw Him use his finger with the blood to trace the letters in my name, Emory Grace Johnson. He said, *'Emory is now my child. Nothing will ever separate us. She is eternally saved from the judgment of her old sin nature. My righteousness is now hers. I have died for all her sins—in her past, in her present, and in her future.'"*

"Then all the angels said. *'Praise to you, all-powerful, all-knowing, ever-present, never-changing Lord. Worthy is the Lamb of God and mighty is the Lion of Judah!'*

"Then I woke up, and I knew that God was for me and that he always will be."

The three adults stood around Emory in stunned silence. Lee was the first to speak, "Emory, that is the most incredible testimony I have ever heard. God has shown his highest favor to you. He has plans for you—plans that are good for you and for his glory."

Pastor Tim and Josie nodded in agreement but remained speechless. The congregation ended their celebration, and the service closed.

As Emory rode home with her parents, she was exhausted. She had genuinely felt the joy of salvation, but there was that one part of her dream she had not disclosed to anyone. It was the part that kept her a little on edge and fearful to say out loud. She did not understand it, but some part of her allowed a knowledge that it was not good, that it was something dark and dangerous. For Jesus, in his last words of the dream, told his angels that yes, his righteousness belongs to her, *"But we have been petitioned by Satan before Emory was born that he be allowed to sift her. And we have given him permission to do so. And now that Emory knows salvation, the sifting will only intensify."*

Chapter 7

The Adversary

1977, 12 years old

*T*welve years old is one of those awkward, in-between ages. No one knew that better than Emory. It was true in the classroom, on the basketball court, and especially at church. Maybe it was part of being a pastor's child and having heard and been blessed with knowing more about the Bible than most kids her age. Whatever the reasons, she often felt left out, longing to do things with older kids but being held back by artificial barriers. It seemed that kids who were falling behind received all kinds of help, but those who excelled were left to fend for themselves at best and uncaringly stifled at worst.

Once again, she sat in the children's class, and once again, she felt bored and out of place. Down the hall, in the Teen Center, she knew her dad had arranged for a movie night for the youth, and she ached to be with them. The unrest stirred her to action. When the teacher was not watching, she slipped out of the room and scurried down the hall.

When she reached the Center, she could hear that the movie had just started. Unnoticed, she sat in the back and watched.

"Hi, my name is Walter French, and the docudrama you are about to see is a fictionalization of creation, the rebellion of Satan, and the consequences to mankind. While it is fictional, it is also biblical, and it is our prayer that the viewer will realize after watching this film that we have an enemy called Satan, but our God is greater than he is. I will be your occasional narrator, so come and let us see how amazing our Lord, whose divine name is Yahweh, truly is."

Emory watched with great expectation as the screen went black and slowly transformed into a starry night sky. Then a beautiful garden appeared, and the night was transformed to day. There was no sun, but the light was searing. A radiant choir of heavenly hosts filled the garden. They were clothed in white robes, and the purity of their songs filled her heart as she watched and listened to them worship in the presence of Yahweh.

"Glory and power and honor are yours, O Lord. We bow before you, for you are worthy of all honor and glory and praise. You are Yahweh, and there is none like you. Hear the praises we bring. For nothing else matters but to glorify you and you alone."

The camera zoomed from a panoramic view to focus on a single heavenly angel. It was obvious that he was the leader. They called him Lucifer, and he was more beautiful than all of the others. He played every musical instrument before him in perfect tone and pitch. This Lucifer personified beauty not only in his appearance, but even in his voice. He turned and faced the throne to sing and bow before the Lord. Then he spoke:

"Lord, our creator, you are Yahweh. We have gathered to serve you as you desire. I am honored to lead this choir and bring all of this great praise before you.

Now we ask you to speak so we may know your plans and the commands you have for us."

Emory gulped hard and waited as a great hush fell over the multitudes and the angels all knelt before the throne. The throne never appeared on the screen, but the light coming from it was blinding. Walter's voice explained why. "The holiness of God on his throne cannot be looked upon by anyone. To do so would mean death. While unseen, please listen carefully to the great announcement of Yahweh."

"It is my desire to create a new world. This place will have a sun and moon and stars and shall exist in a distinct place I have marked for it. On the dry land, I shall display my glory and splendor in the beauty of the flowers and trees. The birds I will teach to sing and soar in the expanses of the sky. I shall make all sorts of animals, tall and short, spotted and striped, swift and strong. I shall populate the great oceans, raging rivers, babbling brooks, and still ponds with living creatures, suitable for the water. All of these living things will thrive in the divine nature and plans that I have established.

"And I shall also create man, and I will give him a helpmate, woman. They will be my crowning jewels created in my very own image. All these other things I have made will be for their enjoyment and good pleasure. They shall live in a perfect garden, freely walking with me. They shall have no need of anything, for I shall provide and care for them. They shall be so close to me that they will reflect my glory."

An eruption of praise and enthusiasm filled the air. Angels marveled at their leader. Then the most unexpected of all, Yahweh quickly calmed them by his unspoken command. A silence teeming with expectation followed. Yet there was a twinge of, what was it, foreboding? Yahweh's voice was directed at Lucifer. It was a voice of authority, of knowing, or more accurately of judgment.

"Lucifer."

"Yes, my Lord?"

"Lucifer, I have created you in beauty and given you many talents. I have placed you at the highest echelon of my army and honored you with leadership ability and intellect."

"Yes, Lord, you have given all these to me, and I have stewarded them well for you. Is it not I who leads the hosts of angels in all worship of you?"

"Indeed, you have stood in front of all who worship, but I find you lacking and impure in your motives. Lucifer, I know your every intention, so speak now, and conceal no longer your true agenda. Vocalize your plans for all to hear. You cannot hide them from me, and now I command you to speak. Your stewardship is stained. You have become corrupt so say it to me in the presence of these."

A view of Lucifer dominated the screen. Emory studied his face and held her breath waiting for his response, for he had been called out by the very Creator of all. He snarled his lip and stood taller. With a clenched fist and crimson face, the morning star prepared to deliver his response. She could tell that he would hold nothing back, and a sense of delight seemed to filter through his beautiful essence.

"Very well, Yahweh, may it be as you say. I will hide no more from you or from this angelic host my ambition, and I shall proclaim loudly and proudly that which I deserve. I now claim that which is rightfully mine and what you have withheld from me. I will

*ascend into the heavens and claim my highest posi-
tion, which I have earned through my own work and
strength. No longer just the morning star, I shall be
the star of stars. I will be idolized, and glory shall be
given to me by all creation. Even the creation of those
you call man. I will usurp your power and take your
place, for you have taken me for granted and held
back the things that I deserve. I will be taking a multi-
tude of these angels who stand here behind me, and
they shall forever be my followers, not yours."*

Emory sat with rapt attention to everything being
played out before. She knew the story of creation but
had never heard how rebellious Satan was before the
world was even made. "No wonder Satan is bound
for hell," she whispered and leaned in to hear more.

The light emanating from the throne began to pul-
sate and intensify. The angels backed away from the
hot light—all of them except Lucifer, who stood defi-
ant and audacious before the Lord. Yahweh's booming voice delivered the judgment:

*"You have spoken truly of your desire, Lucifer, for
all that you have said I have known from the origin
of such thinking within you. You have forgotten that
I am God, and there is none who is my equal. You
seek to steal my glory and claim it for your own. But
what you fail to comprehend is that I alone am holy,
and my glory is my essence. Because of your pride,
you shall drink from the cup of my wrath. You shall
no longer be called Lucifer, and the shining star that
you are will no longer shine with the luster I gave you
on the day I made you. Instead, your name will be
Satan, and you will no longer reside in heaven. There
is no place here for your darkness."*

"You tell him, Yahweh!" Emory mouthed.

45

"Tell me then, Lord, where shall I live, and what powers will I retain?"

"Your presumptions are a stench in my nostrils, Satan. That I should continue to allow your existence is more than you deserve, but I will allow you to continue in your ways. In the future, you will even be allowed to return momentarily to these heavens to seek my permission for the evil that you will conspire to use against me and my creation. I shall cast you out into darkness until the time of the earth's creation. Then I will allow you to live among the man I will create."

The screen showed a cataclysmic explosion erupting and spewing ash and multicolored flames in every direction. An invisible force moved all of the Lord's angels to the right of the throne. A powerful gale blew the rest into Satan's arena, where the ash and flames intensified and gradually became denser and darker.

"Whoa!" Emory said a little too loudly. She looked up to see if her dad or anyone else had heard her, but it looked like everyone was as enmeshed in the film as she had been. "Go on, Yahweh, give it to him," she whispered.

"Satan, take these dark demons from my sight. I cast you out of heaven and into a realm in which you shall no longer have a relationship with me. You shall forevermore be my adversary. Yet I will allow you to do much to pursue your lust and pride; but know this, no matter what you do, I am still and always sovereign. You shall be used, even in your evil ways, to glorify me."

Emory was thrilled by what she was watching. To visualize God putting Satan in his place was an inspiration. She thought the film was over, but Walter, the narrator, interrupted her preparations to leave.

"We do not know how much time passed before the next scene actually occurred. What matters is the truth of what you will now witness. Let's return again to hear Yahweh speak to his followers."

"My faithful ones, your former brother, Satan, is intent on corrupting and perverting my created man and woman. He will rise up against them to kill, steal, and destroy them. The relationship I desire to have with mankind will be severed. In so doing, Satan will also corrupt nature and the world I have made."

Satan's defiance of God and hatred for people was unbelievable to Emory. Remembering her former mistake, Emory whispered, "No wonder he is called our enemy. He is just pure evil."

"Satan deserves your full and complete punishment, Lord. Destroy him and preserve all the good things you have created."

Emory nodded in the affirmative, "I agree with the angels, God. Why don't you just get rid of this horrible creature?"

"No, my angels. I have plans for Satan. He will be taken care of justly, but I will soon call upon you for new assignments with regard to man. In the course of time, you shall be guardians and protectors as well as messengers to reveal truth. This man and woman are not like you. They will have little understanding of the spiritual realm and the battles fought here. Yet, through man, my glory will be enhanced, and Satan will be used by me to prove my love and righteousness and power. Even Satan will confess one day that I am the only true, living God."

"Praise you, our Lord. You are wise beyond our comprehension; may man see your truth."

Yahweh reassured his angels, "Do not be afraid, but wait and watch how I will take all things and work them together for the good of all those who love me and are called according to my purposes. Man and woman will fail me and fall short of my glory. But then I will do the unthinkable. I will send my Son to redeem these people and my Spirit will one day indwell those who believe in me and my Son's sacrifice for them. No power will ever snatch those believers from me, for greater is He that will be in them than he that is in this world I have made. My word is eternal and will not return void."

The voices of the angels grew louder: *"Praise Him from whom all blessing flow."*

The heavenly scene faded, and Walter reappeared. "Well, my friends, I pray that you will take this knowledge of the spiritual battle that started before the creation of the world with you. More important, I hope that as you face struggles and temptations, you will understand that Satan is your enemy, and God is always for you. The Bible tells us there is a spiritual realm that we cannot see and that the war for our souls will not end until Christ returns. So be ever watchful for the lies and distortions of this world and cling to the Truth, Jesus Christ. Please do your part to be ready when the enemy rises up against you. We all must continue to pray and study God's Word. Remember, Jesus himself was tested by the devil, and Satan fled from him when Jesus stood on the Word of God."

Emory's heart was beating like it did when she ran wind sprints in basketball practice. The joy of her salvation was bumped into turbo drive. She wanted to sing like the angels did. She looked around and saw others getting up and moving around. Knowing the lights would come on soon, she made it to the door just in time.

Chapter 8
Unwanted Discovery

1978, 13 years old

*W*ednesday night was a big night at the Teen Center, and Emory was a regular fixture there. She loved the new youth minister's assistant, Lynn Dalton, and looked forward to seeing her more than anything else. Tonight was going to be great because her dad was covering for Pastor Tim in prayer meeting. That meant that Lynn would be doing the entire program by herself.

Emory worked feverishly to finish her homework, take Pepper for his daily walk, and then feed him. She rushed into the house, traditional door slam included, and shouted to her dad, "Come on, Dad, I want to get there early to help Lynn with the setup."

"Okay, okay, let's go."

Lee drove to the Center as Emory talked non-stop. "Tonight, we are studying the book of Genesis. I'm not sure which part, but all of Genesis is good."

"Couldn't have said it better, my daughter."

"Dad, do you know anything about Lynn? I really like her."

"I think she is twenty-two or twenty-three, and she just got married a year ago. I believe she played a year of basketball at the University of Georgia."

"Really, she likes basketball, too?"

"Oh, yes. I understand she is quite good. She only played a year because women's sports were just getting started then."

"Wow! That is so cool."

"I'm sure if she has time, she can teach you a few basketball moves."

"Really, think I can ask her tonight?'

"Sure, but Emory, you need to respect her time. Don't be disappointed if she can't help you out. She is new here and has a lot going on."

"Don't worry, Dad. I'll just ask her nicely, and whatever she says will be fine with me. Doesn't hurt to ask, as you always say."

"I am impressed and flattered that you listen and quote your old dad."

"Dad, you are funny. You know I listen."

"Yes, Emory, you are a good daughter."

"You're not so bad yourself!"

They were still laughing when Lee parked in his reserved space. Emory unbuckled her seat belt and opened the door before he could put the car in park.

"Emory!" her dad exclaimed in mock panic.

"See you later, Dad," she shouted back.

"Love your enthusiasm," he responded.

Pushing through the exterior doors, Emory bounded down the corridor and turned right into the Teen Center. Scouting the gym, she did not see Lynn anywhere. She tried the kitchen area next. Bingo, there she was, sitting at a table just outside the kitchen door. She appeared to be reading something.

Running to the table, Emory smiled when Lynn looked up. She was so pretty with a deep tan and jet-black hair. She wore a pair of jeans and a polo shirt with the Teen Center emblem on it. Why did it look so much better on her than on anyone else?

"Hey, Lynn, I tried to get here early tonight to see if you needed any help with anything."

"Well, thank you, Emory. That was so thoughtful of you. I think the boys have already gotten all the tables set up, so we are good."

Disappointed but undeterred, Emory sat down next to Lynn. Just being near her was a pleasure. "So, Lynn, my dad tells me you played basketball in college."

"Your dad speaks the truth, Emory, but only a year."

"But that is so neat, Lynn. You are like a pioneer."

"Well, I've never been called a pioneer before, but I guess it's true. Not sure how much I like it, though. It makes me feel really old."

"No, Lynn. It's a compliment, an honor."

"Well, thank you, Emory. Do you play?

"I love basketball. I'm hoping to be good enough to play in college one day too. But they don't have any teams for girls my age around here yet. I tried to get on one of the boys' teams, but they wouldn't let me. I don't know why. I'm better than most of those boys. Those boys think they are so good."

"Hmm, do you feel like that isn't fair, Emory?"

"Yes, I do. How am I going to get any better if I don't play against some good competition?"

"You play pick-up games here. I've watched you, and you are pretty good."

Emory felt a strange flutter in her heart. Lynn had watched her. Not only that, she had given her approval of Emory's ability.

"You think so?"

"You hold your own against those boys."

53

"Yes, but they either let me win, or they bully and foul me constantly. I can't have a competitive game with them."

"I see. Well, I think we have a little time. Want to play a one-on-one game to ten baskets?"

"Really?"

"Let's see what you got, Emory. Shoot to see who gets the ball first."

"Bam, nailed it! I get first possession. Are we playing 'make it, take it'?" Emory asked.

"Of course you would ask that since you have the ball," Lynn laughed.

Emory shrugged, "It's a game of strategy, too."

"All right, 'make it take it.'"

For twenty minutes, Emory played hard against her newly found idol. This game was the first time ever in her competitive life that she didn't care if she won or lost. It was Lynn's attention that fed her malnourished soul, and twenty minutes was over far too quickly.

Winded but jubilant, Emory grabbed the ball as it passed through the net on Lynn's final shot. "Whew, good game, Lynn. That was great."

"It was fun to get back out on the court again. I was rusty, but I guess I still got a little left."

"Well, you beat me ten to seven, but you do have a couple of inches on me."

"Emory, you have great potential. You keep working, and you will reach that college goal of yours."

"Thanks, Lynn. Can we play again sometime?"

"Sure, maybe we can even talk some guys into playing us two-on-two."

"That would be great!"

They looked up as about a dozen teens walked into

the gym. The church van must have just arrived with the community kids.

"Oh my goodness, they are here. I need to look at my lesson plan some more. Not sure if I'm ready yet."

"You will do fine, Lynn. You always do." *Everything you do is perfect and beautiful.* Emory's thought surprised her, but she did not dismiss it.

Lynn walked to her table and picked up her notes. She moved to the lectern and had all the kids sit at the tables around her. "Okay, everyone. Thanks for coming tonight. Before we do any of our other activities, I am going to lead us in our Bible lesson."

"Tonight, we are going to tackle a subject that may be a little awkward or uncomfortable for some of you. If any of you are embarrassed, I want you to know it's okay. But what is not going to be okay are any snide or crude remarks about tonight's topic, which is sex."

Not surprising, there were rustling sounds and whispers in the audience. A few of the boys laughed nervously, and the girls mostly avoided looking at anyone.

"Okay, now that we have that introduction over, I want everyone's to look up here at me. You are in your teens now, and we in the church are not naive about the things you are exposed to. It is extremely important that you all know the real truth about sex from a biblical perspective."

Emory, like the others, had felt a wave of embarrassment, but now she was fully engaged in Lynn's presentation. She had very little exposure to this topic and was grateful that Lynn and not her dad was teaching her.

Lynn pressed on, "Reading from the New International Version of the Bible in Genesis, Chapter Two, this is what it says:

'The LORD God said, "It is not good for the man to be alone. I will make a helper suitable for him."

'Now the LORD God had formed out of the ground all the wild animals and all the birds in the sky. He brought them to the man to see what he would name them; and whatever the man called each living creature, that was its name.

So the man gave names to all the livestock, the birds in the sky and all the wild animals. But for Adam, no suitable helper was found.

'So the LORD God caused the man to fall into a deep sleep; and while he was sleeping, he took one of the man's ribs and then closed up the place with flesh.

'Then the LORD God made a woman from the rib he had taken out of the man, and he brought her to the man.

'The man said, "This is now bone of my bones and flesh of my flesh; she shall be called 'woman,' for she was taken out of man."

'That is why a man leaves his father and mother and is united to his wife, and they become one flesh.

'Adam and his wife were both naked, and they felt no shame.'"

Lynn continued with her commentary on the Scripture. "What the Lord says here is crystal clear. He does not mince words. Let me paraphrase it for you. He says, 'I have seen to it that man has all his heart longs for, and I have provided a helpmate for him—a woman. I have set the standard that man and woman shall become one flesh in covenant marriage, and they have received my command to be fruitful and multiply. I have stated clearly that this is my intention for man and woman and this is my absolute will. Man shall never lie with anyone but woman, and woman shall lie only with man. All other knowledge of flesh is absolutely forbidden."

"The world is going to offer you some alternatives to this standard. Yes, sex is a gift from God, but it is a gift to be experienced only in marriage as God has prescribed."

"I know that soon you all will start dating. Some of you may already be doing so. You need to be aware that temptations will come. It will be easy to give in to the desires in your body. People and television and the songs you listen to are going to tell you it is good and right to have sex with anyone you feel like you love. The Bible tells us that the heart is full of deceit. That means feelings are going to take you outside of the will of God. Never base any important decision solely on feelings. Get wisdom and power from God's Word.

"Boys, listen to me. Any girl you date, you are to respect. She is made in the image of God just like you are. You are not to pressure her or give in to any temptation to have premarital sex. And once you are married, you have a covenant with God to be faithful to her always. That means if you cheat on her, you are cheating on God."

"Girls, the same is true for you. If ever you are pressured by a guy, you must lean on the power of the Word. Any boy who says, 'Have sex with me to prove you love me,' is a boy you need to say goodbye to right then and there.

"Any questions?"

Emory sat ramrod straight in her chair. Lynn's words were sound, and she knew the verses well. No emotion at all came to her, having sex with a boy was completely unimaginable. Tonight's lesson would be an easy one for her to live by all her life.

A hand rose from the table of boys who sat behind Emory.

"Yes, Ronnie, do you have a question?"

"Yeah, I do. When do we eat?'

Lynn sighed, a look of futility and hurt crossing her face. Seeing the hurt, Emory's anger rose. She turned and shot a hard look at the boy, "Ronnie, that was so rude."

"No, it wasn't," he retorted. "It was funny." He laughed along with all the boys.

Emory readied herself to get up and teach them a lesson in respect. Seeing the impending conflict, Lynn defused the situation quickly.

"It's okay, everyone. I think we are finished anyway. My last thoughts are that I hope all of you heard what I have shared with you tonight. If there are no serious questions, we can eat now. But listen, this is really important, and the decisions you make about how you use your body will have major consequences for you and for others. God sees all. God knows all, and he has commanded that you use his gift of sex only within the parameters of his standard. Take that with you and live accordingly."

Emory did not move for a few minutes. It took everything she had not to call Ronnie out. He deserved it for being such a jerk to Lynn. But she remembered where she was and that her dad would suffer for her less-than-hospitable behavior. She calmed herself and walked toward Lynn, but Ronnie jumped into her path.

"Say, Emory, what is your problem anyway? It was just a joke."

"Well, it wasn't very funny, Ronnie. Lynn puts a lot of time into being here and teaching us these things, and you thank her by being a complete jerk."

"Okay, okay. I'm sorry."

"Don't tell me. Tell her."

"Why? You are the one that is making such a big deal out of it. She's already let it go. Why don't you?"

"Why don't you just grow up?!"

"Whoa, why all the anger? Why are you so protective of her anyway?"

"I just believe in respect and common courtesy. Look, I don't have time to waste talking to you. Just never be so rude with her again."

Emory stepped around him and continued toward Lynn. She had to tell her how much she had enjoyed the lesson and to console her for the cruel words that Ronnie had thrown at her. As she walked away, she heard one of the girls tell Ronnie something that would ring in her ears for a long time to come.

"Don't worry about her, Ronnie. She is being totally unreasonable. It's like she feels like she has to guard Lynn's feelings. Hmm, guess she has a crush on her or something."

Laughter followed Emory out the door as she walked past Lynn and into a world of questions and confusion.

Chapter 9
Family Fracture

1980, 15 years of age

*E*mory finished making her bed and looked at the books stacked on her desk. That term paper was not going to write itself, but getting started was the hardest part. She had done all the leg work by going to the library and checking out all the books she could find on Benedict Arnold. She had chosen the topic herself because all anyone knew about the man was that he was a traitor to his country. While she did not condone his betrayal or disagree with his punishment, his motivation intrigued her. Why would a patriot turn traitor?

Pepper nuzzled her hand to remind her he was there and needed to be fed. "All right, boy, let's go get breakfast, and then I will take you for a quick walk. Don't be too disappointed that it is short, though. I have to start this paper today because time is short with basketball in full swing. Let's go, boy."

The duo bounded down the stairs, Pepper's tail wagging in anticipation of the treats to come. At the bottom of the stairs, Emory stopped short. It sounded like some kind of serious conversation was going on with her family, but she was not invited to be a part of it. Growing more and more curious and feeling left out yet again, she decided to eavesdrop.

Eva was talking, "Mom, Dad, listen to me, please. I know that this was not my plan in high school. I know that you are very disappointed, but I have almost a year of college already completed, and I can always go back later. Right now, all I want to do is be with Rick. We love each other so much. Surely you remember how you felt at my age. I have to go with him, and we cannot wait. The army is sending him to his first duty station, and I'm going with him. Dad, please don't look at me that way."

Emory peeked around the corner and saw her dad looking at his oldest daughter. Tears welled up in his eyes as he pleaded with Eva.

"I'm sorry, honey, it's just that I can still remember the day we brought you home from the hospital. Our first-born baby girl. I remember your first steps, your first words. Being your dad was the most amazing day in my life."

Emory's stomach turned. *Sure, Dad, wonder if you would say those things about your second born. I know Mom wouldn't, but you, I'm not sure.*

"Eva, I know you are pretty much a grown woman now."

"Not pretty much, Dad, I am."

"Yes, you are a beautiful grown woman. But you are still young with a lifetime ahead of you. Rick can go ahead of you and get settled. Please just resist the impulse to go now. He will wait for you if it is true love."

"Dad, we already know it is true love. This is not a whim. We have been dating for two years. We know it's right for us. Please, Dad, will you and Mom just give us your blessing?"

Emory could tell her mom was trying to steady

herself so she could speak. *Oh, this should be pretty mushy.*

"Eva, we love you, sweetheart. That's why we are trying so hard to help you see this is not a good decision. The army is going to be a whole new life for Rick. Eva, you know we have a few reservations about Rick, but we do not dislike him. He needs to mature and handling a new career and a new wife all at once may overwhelm him. Think about how hard all these adjustments will be for him all at once. It seems that the best way to help Rick would be to wait and let him take a few steps at a time."

Eva, what are you thinking? The guy is an idiot. All guys are just users.

"No, Mom, you are wrong. You and Dad just don't get it. I will be there to help him begin his career. If we are married, the army will let him live in married housing instead of those awful barracks. I can cook him real meals and make sure his uniform is pressed. We will be partners together in all this new exciting life. Now is the perfect time to get married."

And you want to sell yourself into slavery? Maybe you are an idiot, Eva. Why do you have to be so weak and dependent on this guy?

Emory watched as her mom and dad exchanged long looks of anguish and resignation. It was written all over their faces. They were going to cave into Eva like they always did.

Lee's voice was awash with emotion. "Eva, your mother and I have often talked about what your wedding day would be like. I always thought I would walk you down the aisle to give you away and tell the young man he had better take good care of you. Your mother's visions were full of all the preparations with flowers and food and, of course, the wedding gown. Most of all, we wanted so much to see your joyful smile as you walked to the man you had chosen to spend your life with. We will not have any of that now that you have decided to go away like this."

"Dad, please, you know I love you both, and I wanted that too, but things are just happening that I can't change. If I could do it differently, I would. Of course, I would want you both to be there. I would want to dance with you and have pictures taken with you and all that. Look, this is just one event in my life. I know it is one of the biggest, but there will be other times we can celebrate together."

"Eva, I will say only this, we will be praying for you and for Rick. I fear that you may not have truly sought God's will in this even though you say you have. Don't worry. I'm not going to lecture you on that. We know your decision is made, and we want you to be happy. We cannot honestly give you our blessings, but we are not angry with either of you. We will miss you so much, and you know you always are welcome here, as is Rick."

"I know this is hard for both of you. Thank you for understanding. I have to go finish packing. Our bus leaves at three. Love you."

With that, Eva hugged Josie, then Lee, and raced toward the stairs. The patter of her feet startled Emory, but there was no time to hide.

"Oh hey, Emory, I guess you heard. Rick and I are getting married! Aren't you excited for me?'

"Why? Why would you want to leave everything you have here to go off with some guy who has nothing to offer you. You have everything here. Mom and Dad do everything for you. Why would you hurt them like this?"

"Emory, I don't expect you to understand, but one day I think you will. When you fall in love, there is no sacrifice you will not make. All of you are selling Rick short. He has ambitions, and he does love me. I refuse to get mad at you right now, Emory, because you just have no way of knowing what it is like. I know this hurts Mom and Dad now, but it is only for a short time. Rick and I will make it up to them later. It isn't easy for me to leave them either, you know. I will even miss you and Pepper, but it is where my heart leads me."

"You are right about one thing. I do not understand this at all. To me, it is just crazy, and I will never let any guy talk me into something as ridiculous as this. But it's your life, so I guess all I can say is good luck."

Eva reached over and touched Emory's shoulder. "Thanks, Emory, and now that I am leaving, you can have my bedroom if you want it. It's a lot bigger than yours."

"Thanks, but I'll keep my own. I have a much better view than you do. Besides, you will be back."

"Emory! You mean you don't think this marriage will work out?"

"No, that's not what I meant. I hope it does work for you and you are very happy. I'd love to have some little nieces and nephews one day. I just meant you would probably come back sometime, you know, just to visit."

"You are probably right. Well, guess I better get busy."

Chapter 10
Abandoned & Vulnerable

Three months later, 16-years-old

*P*epper was really restless for some reason. Emory tried several times to quiet him, but he wouldn't settle. She glanced at the clock. It was just a few minutes before one in the morning.

"Pepper, what is going on with you, boy? You usually sleep like a rock. Well, since I'm awake, let's go downstairs. I'm thirsty for orange juice."

He jumped out of the bed at the invitation and led the way. Still a little groggy, Emory stretched and opened the refrigerator door. She winced at the light and grabbed the bottle of orange juice and some dog treats.

"Here you go, boy." He grabbed the treat and circled the room, finally stopping by the table and sitting down to eat. She followed, not bothering to get a glass. Unscrewing the top, she was about to take a drink when the phone rang. The unexpected noise rattled her. Spilling some of the juice and almost dropping the bottle, she managed to get to the phone after a couple of rings.

She could hear her dad's voice answer the call, and then she recognized that it was Eva calling, crying uncontrollably. Emory strained to understand what Eva was saying through her sobs. She knew

SIFTING EMORY

instantly that this was the phone call her parents had both dreaded and hoped for. Eva needed help. This call was going to end the three months of their longing for her. She was coming back. Emory wasn't sure how she felt about that, but things had changed for her, too, in the last three months. She had a new friend, and all the family neglect of her no longer mattered.

"Dad?"

"Eva?"

"Daddy!"

"Yes, baby, I'm here. What is it? Whatever you need, we are here for you."

"Oh, daddy, please help me. I don't know what to do. Daddy?"

"Yes, darling, we will come to you. Whatever it is, we can take care of it."

"It's Rick, he, he...."

"Listen, Eva honey, just take your time. Tell me about Rick."

"He hit me, Daddy. He hit me! He came in after drinking with his buddies, and I told him he had to stop acting like a child. He got mad and ...."

Her dad's voice was restrained but dripped with boiling anger, "Eva, listen to me. You get out of that house right now. You go to a friend's house or a hotel. You hear me? He will not ever lay a hand on you again, I promise you, baby girl."

Her mother didn't say anything. She never got on the phone, but Emory knew her heart was broken. Finally, Emory heard her in the background burst into tears.

"Oh, Mom, I know how close you are with Eva. This has got to be killing you. Would you be this upset if

it were me? Would you cry for me?" Emory mouthed the words but remained mute.

Her dad eventually regained his composure and spoke with a calm, reassuring voice, "Listen, Eva, it is a seven-hour drive from here to the base. That means I will not be able to get there until about eight or eight-thirty. I want you to meet me at the little coffee shop just outside the front gate—you know the one we ate at when your mom and I came to visit. You and I are going to the commander's office together to take care of this. Then you are coming home with me."

"I can't do that, Dad. I can't get Rick in trouble with his commander. That would devastate him, and I love him. I cannot do that to him. But, please, Daddy, come as soon as you can."

"Going to the commander is a lot better than what I want to do to him, Eva. You just meet me at the shop, and we will talk about everything else then."

"Okay, Dad. Dad, I'm so, so sorry."

"Nothing to be sorry about, sweetheart. You have done nothing wrong. We love you, Eva. Do you think you can find a safe place away from Rick tonight? Where is he now?"

"Yes, there is a friend who will help me. Rick is passed out on the bed. I'm leaving now. Dad, I love you, and tell Mom ..."

"I will, Eva. I will. You be safe, and I will see you soon."

As soon as they hung up, Emory went upstairs and put Pepper in her room. Then she went to her parents' bedroom door and was trying to decide if she should knock. Instead, she just stood there and listened. She could hear them both crying.

Finally, her dad said, "Babe, I've got to change and hit the road right away to get there by eight. I don't want to be late for her."

"Wait a minute, Lee. Don't even think that you are going without me."

"Yes, I am, Josie. You need to stay here with Emory and get everything ready because Eva is coming back home."

"I know she is coming home, Lee, and we are going to go get her. I can't sit here for hours and wait. Don't deprive me of seeing Eva again as soon as I possibly can. She needs us both, Lee. She deserves the love and support of both of her parents."

"I cannot argue with that, Josie. She does need us both. What about Emory? What shall we tell her, and who will take care of her while we are gone?"

"You forget, Lee, Emory is sixteen now and very mature for her age. We just tell her that we are going to get Eva to bring her home. She is old enough to stay by herself for the rest of tonight and get to school tomorrow. They have a game tomorrow at five, and she always likes to ride home with that new girl, Shane. We should be home by seven or eight tomorrow night, so she will not be alone for long."

"What if we get held up and get home later?"

"Then we will call Mrs. Brown next door and have Emory stay with her."

"She's going to be disappointed that we will not be there for her game. You know starting on the high school team as a freshman is a pretty big deal, and we never miss a game."

"I know, Lee, but this is an emergency. I think she will understand."

"You're right. Now let's hurry and get dressed. I'll

get the car ready, and you tell Emory what is happening. Josie, be sure and tell her we are really sorry that we will miss her game."

"I will. I am so glad she is not all boy-crazy like Eva was at that age."

Emory scooted quickly to her room and jumped into bed. When her mom knocked, she feigned awakening from a sound sleep and pretended to know nothing.

"Your dad and I hate to miss your game, honey, but this is Eva."

Yeah right, have none of you people ever heard of a bus ticket? Mommy and Daddy to the princess's rescue as usual. That other kid, what's her name, oh yeah, Emory, is fine on her own. Whatever.

Determined to hide her thoughts, she played the happy helper. "It's okay, Mom. I can manage here without you." And she meant it as the walls of her heart closed around her loneliness.

Chapter 11
Shane

"Come on, Emory, let's go! Play a little defense in there. Hands up and slide those feet. Watch the back-door passes."

Coach Radcliff glanced up at the scoreboard. Only fourteen seconds remained. His Rockets still trailed by a point, and the Rangers had the basketball. He ran the scenarios through his head. If they did not get a steal, they were going to have to foul. The Rangers were the best free-throw shooters in the region, and if they hit them both, the game was over. He looked down the bench at the new kid who had just transferred in. Shane was six feet tall and very athletic but had only played volleyball before this year. Her inexperience was evident, but defense was her specialty. Those long arms were deceptive. How many times in practice had some of his best players misjudged her ability to intercept? This situation seemed to fit her skills. She was quick, defensive, and a jumper. As long as she didn't have to dribble or shoot, it might work. He couldn't get her in the game without a timeout, which he couldn't call while the other team had the ball.

The official's whistle blew as the ball flew out of bounds. Great, Emory had managed to kick the ball out of bounds. Couch immediately jumped off the bench signaling for the Rockets' last time out.

"Girls, get over here quickly. Shane, you're in. Get up here."

Every girl looked at Shane astonished—none more shocked than Shane herself. Her six-foot frame stood well above her teammates. With blue eyes big as saucers and adrenaline pumping through her body, she joined her huddled teammates.

"Me, Coach?"

"Yes, Shane, you. Listen to me, everyone, especially you, Shane. This is one of the most important games we have played this year, and Shane, you have not played much. But I would not put you in if I did not think you were our best bet at beating these gals. Is everyone with me?"

"Yes, Coach!" they chimed.

"Okay, Shane, do what you do. Play defense and intercept one of those passes. We are going to double team whoever gets the pass in-bounds, forcing a pass. Shane, you have got to make sure you are the one who gets that pass."

Shane, now fully engaged, answered, "Got ya', Coach."

"Now, Shane, listen carefully; when you get the ball, you have only one thing to do, just like at practice. Emory will be breaking off the double team and running down court. Shane, do not dribble the ball, not once. Pass it down court, and Emory will be open for a layup."

They broke the huddle, and Emory went quickly over to Shane for encouragement. She reached up and put her arm on Shane's shoulder as they took their positions on the court. "You can do this, Shane, and as soon as we win this game, I'll buy you a coke. Oh, sorry, a soda as you call it. Come on, girl."

Emory tapped her on the butt and ran to her spot to defend the in-bound play. Shane stretched her stiff muscles and prepared to make the play for her team, especially for Emory.

The ball was tossed in, as expected, to their best ball handler. Emory and Brittany trapped her in the corner, making sure not to foul. With seven seconds to go, in desperation, the Rangers' player lobbed a pass intended for her open teammate. Shane jumped like she was at the volleyball net again. She touched the bottom of the ball and tipped it to herself. With three seconds to go, Emory raced down the court. Shane hit her with a pass in stride. Emory turned on the jets with a quick dribble, stutter-stepped, jumped, and released the ball in one fluid motion. The ball was in mid-air as the game-ending buzzer sounded. It swished through the net.

Jubilation filled the home gym. The team collapsed into a big sweaty ball of celebrants at mid-court. Coach Radcliff pumped his fist and hugged his players.

The pile of players slowly dispersed into separate groups of pairs and trios. Shane grabbed Emory and embraced her tightly. "Emory, you are awesome—even if you are just a kid."

"No, Shane, you are the awesome one. We could not have done it without you. Man, you can jump! That pass you gave me was beautiful. But listen, don't give me any of that kid stuff even if you are a year older. You are still as green as grass when it comes to basketball."

"Well, I guess you got me there. Maybe you can give me some one-on-one coaching sometime."

"Sure, I'd be happy to, and I guess I owe you a

soda, huh?"

"You better believe you do, and I plan to collect right after we get cleaned up. Say, I know your folks are usually at your games. I'm really sorry they missed you winning it at the buzzer."

"Thanks, Shane. I am a little disappointed they weren't here. All right, I guess I need to get how I really feel off my chest. I am hurt that they weren't here. I really appreciate your thinking of my feelings. You know there is something about you that makes me feel like I can just tell you things I don't tell other girls."

"Come on now, you know it's just because I'm super cool, and I'm not so hung up on myself as a lot of the girls around here seem to be. I swear, I know she is my teammate, but if I have to hear Ann whine one more time about her cheating boyfriend, I think I'll hit her. Just drop him already!"

Emory laughed, fully appreciating Shane's sentiments. "Oh my gosh, I know what you mean, and they are all that way. I guess that's why Pepper has been my best friend all these years. You know, until you moved here, I didn't feel like I had a real friend. What is really crazy is that I have only known you two months, and I feel closer to you than anyone in my life—even my own sister."

"Same here. You know, out in California where I used to live, the girls were the same way. The day my dad came in and said we were moving, he was really worried about how I would take it. I just told him to let me know when I needed to start packing. I mean, there was some pretty cool things to do there, and I was disappointed when I found out there was no girls' volleyball team here, but I did not leave any friends back there. Heck, I didn't even have a Pepper. Your dog sounds like he is so neat; I can't wait to meet him. I may even steal him from you if he is as cool as you say."

"Oh, you will meet him all right, and anytime you come over, I will be glad to share him with you. But you will never take him from me. We need each other."

"Deal. Hey, what you say we skip the shower here at school. We can clean up at our houses. I'm ready to go celebrate now. I just saw Coach wave, and looks like no post-game talk. Grab your stuff and let's go."

"I'm game; thanks again for the ride. One day when I'm old like you and have my driver's license, I'll return the favor. For now, with Mom and Dad so caught up in Eva's drama, I'm kind of an orphan."

"Pay it no mind, little orphan Emory. Shane will take care of you. Maybe I'll even teach you a few California party moves."

"Better buckle my seatbelt."

"You have no idea. Let's go party beach style."

As soon as Emory shut Shane's car door, she remembered her home situation again. "Oh my gosh, Pepper! Shane, I'm really sorry, but I need you to take me home. No one has been there to let Pepper out and feed him. I can't believe I forgot him."

"Shoot, I really wanted to show you how to party tonight."

"What?"

"Relax, Emory, I am only kidding. Sure, we will go take care of Pepper. I love dogs. Look, it's only a little after seven. I'm sure he is fine, but he will be happy to see you."

"Shane! Yes, you had me going there for a minute. Hey, I doubt if my folks will be back yet. Do you think you could hang out with me for a while? We have my mom's famous leftover beef stew, and I owe you a coke."

"Sounds great. I'm starving. You would not believe what an appetite I worked up in those ten seconds I played."

"Ha! You are so funny, Shane. I think I have laughed more with you than anyone ever in my life."

"You, my friend, have a superior sense of humor if you laugh at my jokes. It's either that or you just need to get out more."

"I know you are joking, Shane, but there is truth in that. I don't get out very much."

"Why is that, Emory? Are your parents that strict with you? I mean, I know how you have told me they are so involved in the church and all."

"No, it's not really that they are strict. I've just never asked them if I could do stuff very much. The real reason is that I've never had anyone to do things with."

"Well, you do now. We are going to have so much fun together. We can hike and go out to eat or go to a movie or even just listen to music together."

"What about church? Would you like to come with me sometime?"

"Sure, I will find a way to work that one in, too. You know my folks separated a few years ago. Since I've been living with my dad, we have not gone to church. Sundays are football and beer for Dad. Don't get me wrong. He is a great guy. It just really hurt him when Mom left us."

"How about you? She hurt you, too, didn't she?"

"It's been four years since she left, and no one has

ever asked me that question. Everyone called and supported Dad; I was completely forgotten in the shuffle. But, yeah, Emory, it hurts me every day. Not sure I want to talk about it anymore. You don't know how much it took for me to even say that. I'm not even sure why I did. I have become a very guarded person since my mom left. I didn't have friends because I did not want any. I was too scared to get close to anyone, I guess. That's enough of that. How about you? Tell me about your family."

"Not much to tell, really. Dad quit his management job several years ago to become the associate pastor and youth director at Calvary Community Church. We just passed it a couple of blocks back. Mom is mostly a homemaker but works part-time at the church Teen Center."

"What happens at the Center?"

"Let's see, there is a gym and some video games. They also have a workout area and a soda fountain. It's really just a place to hang out. Most of the kids come from some pretty bad homes. They get free meals, and there are people to talk with if the home life is really bad."

"So, they counsel kids."

"Yes, and they try to give them alternatives from things they should avoid."

"You mean like drugs and drinking and sex. That kind of stuff?"

"Exactly."

"Emory, what do you think about all those things?"

"I think there is no place in my life for them. I've grown up in a Christian home, and Jesus is my Lord. So, if I love Him, I will obey Him and not do things that would disappoint Him."

"Oh."

"What is it, Shane? Did I say something wrong?'.

"No, no, not at all, Emory. I'm just, well, I just feel..."

"Whatever it is, Shane, you know you can tell me anything."

"Yes, I know I can, Emory. You are such a good person with such a good family. I'm just not sure you should hang around with somebody like me."

"My goodness, what are you talking about, Shane? You are a great person. I love spending time with you and don't think for a minute my family is perfect. Believe me, we have problems—just like this whole thing with Eva right now."

"What do you mean?

"Well, I wasn't going to tell anyone about this because it is hurting my mom and dad so much, but Eva has really screwed up. She is technically an adult now, so this grown-up sister of mine decides she wants to drop out of college and get married. The guy joins the army and talks Eva into going with him and living on some army post. She just knew her life would be perfect when she married Rick. None of us thought much of him. I mean, I met the guy once and thought 'Loser.'"

Emory sighed deeply, conflicted by her feelings. "To be honest, I didn't think I would miss her because she and I were never close, but, surprisingly, I really kinda do. I think one reason I do is because I see how much my parents miss her. It's sad to see them looking at her bedroom or some old pictures of her when she was a baby."

"The other day, I heard my mom talking to her best friend on the phone about how the weeks had gone by, turning to months. She talked about the empty room, the quietness, the unoccupied chair at the table—all reminders of Eva, who was no longer where she should be. Mom cried when she talked about missing her baking companion and the girl talks. And I know my dad misses always rescuing Eva from mishaps and emergencies with her hair dryer. Every night is the same. I hear them in the kitchen, praying and crying and waiting until their Eva asks for help."

"Wow, Emory, that must be so hard for them and for you to see them so sad."

"As hard as that was, the call they got this morning was heart-wrenching for them. Even though we all expected it, we had no way of knowing it would be this bad. The louse got drunk and hit her."

"Man, bet your parents had a really hard drive with all that weighing on them."

"Shane, they were so hurt and so disappointed. I have never seen my dad without a smile on his face until the day Eva left. My mom just shut down. Then with that call, well, I hope for Rick's sake Dad doesn't get ahold of him. Pastor or not, he loves his girls."

"So, they both went to get her and left you here? I'm surprised your mom left you here. I mean, I understand her wanting to go. Well, it's not my place to say, really."

Emory looked out the car window and wished she did not feel the consuming bitterness in her soul. She didn't want Shane to know that part of her, but the words came anyway,

"Yep, left me here and wished me good luck with our game today. Oh well, you know Eva always told me when we were growing up that she was first-born and first-loved, and it would always be that way. Guess she is right, but that's okay."

"Are you okay, Emory?"

Emory tried to cover her slip of the tongue. She pushed her genuine feelings deep within herself, smiled and lied. "Oh, sure. My parents are great, and I love them very much. If it were me in trouble, they would be there for me. I'm over it, really; no need to waste any more time talking about it. Hey, there's my house. Let's get you and Pepper introduced. Looks like they are not back yet, so we have the run of the house."

Shane pulled into the driveway and turned off her lights. Pepper barked his greeting from inside. Emory grabbed her gym bag and headed in, calling back to Shane,

"Hey, grab your bag. You can shower and change here, and then I will pay up on that soda and even throw in a free meal for you. I will feed Pepper and start warming up the leftovers. Man, I am famished. You can call your dad if you need to since you will be late."

"Yeah, guess I should let him know. I'll do that first."

"Cool, but before you do that, come and meet Pepper."

The furry friend was quick to meet them as the door opened. He jumped up and licked Emory on the face. He then turned to capture Shane's attention. Shane got down and mock-wrestled with him, his tail wagging in pure joy.

"You really are something, boy. Emory, he is just as advertised. No wonder you love him so much. He is just so happy."

"Watch out because it's contagious! You will find yourself smiling every time you see him."

"I can believe it! Come here, boy, let me tug that toy away from you.

Emory laughed, "Okay, you two, that's enough for now. Shane, get a shower so we can eat."

***

"What time is it, Josie?"

"I've got eight o'clock on the nose. You made good time, Lee."

"We did pretty well, but I don't think I will breathe again until I see our Eva."

"Me too, Lee. I know we haven't talked much on this trip, but...."

"I know, Josie. I've been praying, too."

Lee flipped on his turn signal and waited for three cars to come out of the parking lot. Every second that passed seemed like years. Uncharacteristically impatient, Lee drummed his fingers on the steering wheel.

"Come on, come on, people," he muttered under his breath.

Josie reached over and put her hand on Lee's shoulder. She squeezed it warmly but remained silent. He sighed deeply with her touch and gave her a look of relief. The last car finally passed, and he pulled into the first available spot. They got out of the car. Lee extended his hand, and Josie met it gratefully. The Open sign on the glass door clanged loudly with Lee's abrupt entry. Scanning the booths, they did not find her.

Panic welled up in Josie. "Lee, she's not here. Where is she? What should we do? Lee!"

"Relax, honey, it's only eight. I told her it might be eight-thirty. Let's sit down. There's a good booth. We can see the door from there."

As soon as they were seated, the waitress came over to serve them. Neither was interested in what she offered, but they thought they should justify their presence.

"Yes, a couple of black coffees would be good."

"All right, sir, but we do have some really terrific fresh cinnamon rolls."

"No, thank you. Just the coffee, please."

"Coffee it is then. I'll be right back. Sugar and cream are on the table.'

Lee studied the waitress as she walked away. She could not have been more than nineteen or twenty—Eva's age. He thought she was probably working her way through college to be what she has dreamed of being all her life.

"Oh Eva, why did you leave us to come here?" he whispered. He looked at Josie, sobbing quietly on the other side of the table. Her beautiful hair was pulled up on her head, and her deep green eyes betrayed the burden of a mother for a child.

"Josie, honey, what is it?"

"Lee, I'm just being silly. When the waitress mentioned cinnamon rolls, it just made me think of all of the baking Eva and I used to do. I remember she started hanging out in the kitchen as soon as she learned to walk. Her little hands would be right there kneading the dough or mixing the eggs and flour when she was only four. She was very good at it, too, just had that knack."

Josie dabbed her eyes. Thankful for no mascara, she let out a heavy sigh in remembrance of those joyful moments with her little girl.

"Did you know that cinnamon rolls are her favorite? She even made up her own recipe. They were the best, the best cinna..." she could not finish.

The door opened, drawing their attention to it. A lady in her forties walked in with her arm around a younger girl. The girl wore sunglasses and walked gingerly, almost as if she were frightened.

"Eva!" both said together. They quickly got up from the booth and met Eva halfway across the coffee shop. Eva fell into her mother's arms.

"Mom, Dad, I am so sorry. Please forgive me."

"There is nothing to forgive, sweetie. We are here. Everything is going to be okay now," Josie answered.

Eva reached up to remove her glasses, revealing two swollen black eyes and a large cut below her right eyebrow. The cut had apparently been sown together with several stitches. Josie gasped in horror.

"Mom, I'm okay. It hurts, but I've been to the emergency room, and I am fine."

"Mr. and Mrs. Johnson?"

"Oh, I'm sorry. Mom, Dad, this is my friend Lori Cruz. She insisted I go to the hospital, and I stayed with her last night. She's a really good friend."

Lee extended his hand to Lori. "Lori, good to meet you. Thank you so much for all that you have done for our daughter."

"I was glad to help. Why don't we sit down and talk a little? Then I will leave you all alone."

"You're right. Let's do that."

Seated, Lori began again, "I want you both to know you have a very smart and brave daughter. My husband is Captain Henry Cruz, the base chaplain. Together we try to minister to all base personnel. Sadly, domestic abuse is more common than the army wants anyone to know about. It's an ugly side of the stresses put on young men and especially married couples in the service of their country. I've been counseling women for twelve years now; Eva is by no means alone as a victim."

The waitress came back over with coffee and more menus. She placed them on the table and was ready to take their orders.

"Not right now, please."

A little frustrated and confused, the waitress still managed a smile and went back to fill the order. Lee motioned for Lori to continue.

"Eva and I spent most of the night talking, and this is how I know what a remarkable young woman she is. You see, ninety-nine percent of the victims of domestic abuse refuse to file a formal complaint. They say they love the guy; he will change; he is not a bad person—you know, all the lines. What they don't talk about is the harm that has been done not only to their hearts, but also to their souls. The trust they pledged in their wedding vows has been ripped away, and all they feel is blame and fear. So, no complaint is filed. No action is taken, and the cycle continues.

"I'll let Eva tell you what she has decided to do. I am going to leave you now, but if you need anything at all, Eva has my number. Don't hesitate to call me."

Lori stood to leave. Shaking hands with Lee and Josie, she gave Eva a parting hug and left the three to a grateful reunion.

"Quite a friend you've got there, Eva," Lee said.

"Yes, she and Henry are great people. I don't know where I would be without them. She really opened my eyes to a lot of things and helped me to understand that the most loving thing I can do for Rick is to try to get him help. She believes the only way to do that is to report the abuse to the commander. I'm ready to do that now, Dad, and then I just want go home where I belong."

"Yes, home is waiting for you. We have missed you so much, Eva." Josie allowed a half-smile.

"Mom, I have missed you guys, too. One thing I need to make clear to you, though, I am not giving up on my marriage. I love Rick, and I know he loves me. But you were right; he wasn't ready for this yet. He has a lot of growing up to do. Don't worry; I'm not kidding myself into believing I can change him. That's between him and God. I'm just hoping that when he is ready, I can help him along the way."

Chapter 12
Growing Bond

*E*mory stepped quickly out of the shower and half-dried her hair. Throwing on her clothes, she ran down the stairs to get into the kitchen before Shane. She had not intended to take a shower until later, but the smell of herself was not something she wanted to bring to the dinner table, especially with Shane there. She had even used her mom's after-shower spray to smell really good. She didn't really know why, only that her guest might like it.

She was relieved when she reached the kitchen before Shane. Grabbing the leftover stew from the refrigerator, she uncovered it and transferred the contents to a pan.

"Let's see, what would Shane want to eat with it? Bread, yes bread. I think she would like some of the sweet rolls mom just bought. And I know she likes Diet Coke—I owe her one. Is that everything?"

Taking the nicest bowls from the cabinet, she sat them on the table and stirred the stew. Everyone loved her mom's stew, so she was happy there were leftovers. The smell alone made her stomach growl. She took a taste and savored it, wishing for the first time in her life that her mom had taught her how to cook food like this.

Everything was ready except her guest. Glancing at the clock, she wondered what had become of

Shane. Gently ladling the piping hot stew into the bowls and placing the rolls in a basket, she sat everything on the table. Both glasses now filled with ice and Coke, she looked up the stairs and finally yelled up to Shane.

"Hey, you, I'm down here waiting. Dinner is ready. This house is not big enough for you to get lost. Are you about ready?"

Shane appeared at the top of the stairs, her hair still wet. She wore a green sweater that set off her blue eyes and her golden blonde hair.

"I could have given you a hair dryer. Sorry."

"Oh no, that's no problem. I usually just air-dry it anyway. Sorry, it took me so long."

"I didn't mean to rush you. Just checking to see if you were ready to eat."

"Come on, Emory, truth is you just missed me, right? Looks like you got a shower, too."

"Just a splash and dash. I couldn't stand myself any longer."

Shane skipped down the stairs, taking them two at a time, her long legs carrying her with unexpected grace. She slapped her arm around Emory, and together the girls walked into the kitchen.

"Wow! That stew smells amazing."

"Wait until you taste it. It's even better than it smells. People would pay good money for my mom's stew. Everyone says so."

"Great, you even have rolls; and there's that Coke you owe me. Oh, I almost forgot..." Shane held up what appeared to be a piece of notebook paper and handed it to Emory. "This is for you. It's the reason it took me so long up there. I saw the picture of you and Pepper and thought you might like this."

Puzzled, Emory took the paper and gasped in surprised delight. She was looking at a sketched rendition of the photograph that sat on her nightstand.

"Oh, Shane, I don't know what to say. It's incredible. You just did this while you were up there? You were able to draw this that quickly?"

"Yep, it's kind of a hobby of mine. Not very many people know I do sketches. It's just my way of working through some of the tough times in my life, I guess."

"I can't believe it is so beautiful. You are so talented. I love it. It is the best gift anyone has ever given me—with the possible exception of Pepper himself."

"Aw, it's nothing really. But I see why you love that dog of yours. He is so sweet, and I can see how loyal he is to you."

"Pepper and I have grown up together. There is no love like that of a dog."

"Yeah, I had a dog once, too, but mom took him with her. I'm not sure why she had to make my hurt that much deeper. Truthfully, sometimes I think I missed Tonto more than my mom."

Shane hesitated in thought for only a moment and then shot a smile at Emory. Moving toward the table, she sat down and took a sip of her Coke.

"Just what I needed. Come on, let's eat before the stew gets cold."

Emory smiled back, knowing how deeply wounded her new best friend must be and wanting desperately to help her. Most people only saw the tough exterior that Shane portrayed, but Emory saw more, a lot more. It would take time to gain her trust, but she was certain this bond they had was like none she had ever known.

"Yes, let's eat, but first, let's pray and ask God to bless this food."

"Oh, sorry, guess I'm not used to praying before meals. Be patient with me, Emory. I need to brush up on my manners."

"Don't be silly, Shane. We don't stand on formalities in this house. Now give me your hand."

"My hand?

"Yes, we hold hands when we pray. Are you okay with that?"

"Sure, I guess so."

The touch of Shane's hand sent unexpected ripples through Emory's body that were both strange and wonderful. This was the hand that drew the most amazing sketch, the hand she had shared high fives with a hundred times, the hand she didn't want to ever let go of, the hand she hoped would hold hers forever. She hesitated to regain her composure and began to pray,

"Heavenly Father, we thank you for the food we are about to eat and pray that it will nourish our bodies. We pray tonight for Eva and my mom and dad that you will see them home safely. And Father, I thank you that you have brought Shane into my life. I pray for her and for her dad that you will protect them and shine your love into their lives. In Jesus' precious name, we pray, Amen."

"Amen," Shane whispered and held on to Emory's hand.

Emory looked at Shane and did not release her hand either. Shane shook her head a little and cleared her throat.

"Emory, uh, no one has ever prayed for me before. I've never had anyone care for me as much as you do. I have to be honest. I don't know what to do with that—with you. You make me feel like I matter to you."

"Of course, you matter to me. I have not stopped thinking about you since the first day I saw you at school. I can't explain it, but I knew that first day you were different—in a good way. There was just some kind of, I don't even know what to call it, but something made me know I wanted to get to know you."

Shane pulled her hand away and shrugged, "Yes, I know. I have that effect on most people."

Her feigned humor was something that Emory was becoming accustomed to by now. She was beginning to know she should go with the intended deflection. She also was learning how to counter punch.

"Well, the new girl's pretty stuck on herself, isn't she? I hear that most California girls have quite the chip on their shoulders. Now, let's dig in."

They laughed and did just that.

***

Josie shifted her position in the car seat and glanced back at Eva, sleeping at last in the back seat. It had been quite a day, and she was completely depleted. Her gaze went from daughter to her husband. Lee looked so determined yet so exhausted. She had offered twice to relieve him from driving, but he had refused. Finally, she gave up, realizing that he needed to feel in control of something right now, even if it was their old Chevy.

Josie checked the time. It was already eight-thirty, and by her estimation, they were still a couple of hours from home.

93

"Lee, do you think we should stop and call Emory to let her know our status?"

"What? Oh, sorry, Josie, I was a million miles away in my thoughts. Yes, we need to give her a call, and we could all use a break from sitting. There is an exit about two miles up the road. We can call from a gas station. You know, one day, they are going to make those portable phones affordable for folks like us. Won't that be great?"

Josie laughed, "Lee, you come up with the craziest thoughts, but I need to laugh. It feels good."

He smiled at her, "It does, doesn't it? Don't worry, Josie, pretty soon we will be home. I can't wait for you and Eva to get on one of your famous baking frenzies. You know, I am always available as your taste tester."

***

"Emory, that was the best meal I have had in my entire life!"

"And the best company?'

"Goes without saying. By the way, you know you are getting worse than I am on those high self-opinions."

"I've learned from the best."

"Let me help with the dishes."

"Are you kidding? If my mother knew that I let a guest in her house do dishes, she would have my head. Just carry them to the sink, and I'll do them really quickly. Why don't you and Pepper go in the living room and find something good on TV? I'll be right there."

"All right, you win. Come on, boy."

Emory watched her two buddies walk away and

turned quickly to do the dishes. She finished in a flash, doing only a passable job. From what she could hear, it sounded like Shane had settled on some sort of musical station. She walked in just in time for Shane to jump up and pull her in front of the television.

"Come on, we have to do this part with them. "It's fun to stay at the Y-M-C-A. Yes, the Y-M-C-A..."

They were dancing and laughing so hard Emory barely heard the phone ring. She wiped the tears from her eyes and walked to the kitchen.

"Hello?"

Shane rolled over on the coach and began to play with Pepper. She did not want to leave but knew her dad would be expecting her home soon. She could hear Emory's half of the phone call.

"Hi, Mom, how are you all?"

"Sure, that's no problem. You remember Shane, don't you? Well, she gave me a ride home, and I convinced her to stay for dinner."

"Yes, her dad knows that she is still here and it's okay with him, but she has to leave soon. Everything is fine. I will see you when you get home."

"Okay, be careful. Bye."

Shane peeked around the corner, "So the family is good?"

"Yes, they will be home in an hour or two, and Eva is with them."

"Good, I'm glad. Guess I better be heading home. Dad will need to hear about our big win today."

"Our win, that's right. You know the strangest thing just happened?"

"What's that?"

"Mom did not even ask me about the game. They

knew it was a huge deal to me, and she did not even ask. But that's not the strange thing. The strange thing is that it did not even bother me that she didn't. I think sharing it with you filled that void. Anyway, it just did not bother me in the slightest. Thank you for that."

"Not exactly sure what I did, but I'm glad I could help out. Emory, thank you for the best night I've had in a long time. Let's do it again sometime."

"You're on. See you tomorrow. Be safe driving home. Will you call me when you get there?"

"What do you think? Am I that bad of a driver?"

"No, just want to make sure you get home. I can't have anything happen to my teammate. Coach always says we gotta' look out for each other."

"Sure, I'll give you a call. You didn't even have to ask."

Chapter 13
The Fight

$\mathcal{T}$he Teen Center was bustling. Kids ate free pizza and ice cream as others played games. The biggest hit seemed to be the basketball court, where a clinic was taking place.

Lee walked into the Center and was amazed and thankful. It was a slow start in the beginning, but word of mouth had brought in kids from all over—kids he knew who needed a place like this. It was indeed a sanctuary for many. He smiled as kids got to be kids here, and Bible stories were a part of every teen's presence at the Center.

As he approached the basketball court, his smile broadened. He could not help but be proud of how Emory and her friend, Shane, had started the clinic on their own initiative.

He looked long at Emory and knew that he had an exceptional daughter. She was the kindest person he knew and the most selfless. Looking at her on the court, he was a little in awe of her athletic abilities. Unlike Eva, he was sure that college and a scholarship were in her future.

"Belle, that was a good pass, but you need to step toward the person you are passing it to so that it gets to your teammate and not the other team. Okay? And the same goes when you are getting the ball passed to you. Go out and receive the ball.

"Okay, Emory, and if they foul me, I get a free shot, right?"

"Right."

Lee laughed at the great progress being made in the youngsters. At their age, ranging from six to ten, they were so coachable. He moved his eyes to the other side of the court to watch Shane.

"Got it, Coach Shane. Like this?" Young Freda dribbled the ball twice with her fingertips and looked at Shane. Then she stopped and dribbled again.

Shane laughed and hit herself in the head. "Yes, Freda, exactly like that, but I forgot to tell you about the rule that will not allow you to double dribble."

"Do what? This game sure does have a lot of rules."

The clock buzzer sounded, ending the day's session. By the look on Shane's face, it was perfect timing.

Emory blew her whistle and announced, "Okay, everyone put all the stray basketballs on the rack and come to center court."

The kids scurried to obey, vying to be the first to the center. Without further instructions, they formed a large care circle and joined hands. Black, white, and brown hands entwined in a priceless picture of trust and unity. Eyes closed and heads bowed, they prayed in unison.

"Father, we give you thanks for all the good things you provide. We know that you love us, and you want us to love one another. Help us to be everything you want us to be. In Jesus' name, we pray. Amen."

As the circle broke, they raced to the kitchen area for take-home snacks. Lee watched the hungry and grateful hands snatch up the goody bags, every kid saying, "thank you." He knew that most of the kids would end up sharing their snacks with younger siblings at home and wished he could do more. Still, he breathed a prayer of gratitude that the Lord had enabled them to have this ministry and how he had built it to what it was today.

"Hey, Dad, so did you get to see any of the clinic that Shane and I are putting on?"

Lee turned and saw the two sweaty coaches standing behind him. Laughing, he said, "I sure did, and I must say I was very impressed. Those kids have come such a long way in just a few days. I can tell they really love their coaches."

"I am just glad to finally find someone who dribbles worse than I do, Mr. Johnson."

Emory laughed and punched Shane on the shoulder, "Give them another week, and even they will be better than you."

"Very funny, you wise guy."

"Well, all I know is that they love it, and I really cannot tell you how much I appreciate you two taking your time to help out around here."

"Dad, you know we love this game. And before we did this, I never knew how much I liked working with kids—but only in sports, I don't want the rest of their drama."

Shane nodded in agreement then turned to Lee, "Mr. Johnson, I should be thanking you for the opportunity. You and your whole family have made me feel really at home here."

"Shane, you are like part of the family, and you are welcome any time. Now, I've got a meeting to get to about raising more funds for this place. Emory, you want to wait for me to take you home?"

"No thanks, Dad. Shane and I are going to the mall

for a little while then she will give me a ride home. I'll see you at home."

"Okay, thanks again. See you soon. Love you."

"Love you too, Dad. Well, Shane, let's get going."

"Do you know how much I love being your chauffeur?"

"No, but I know I sure like it."

Shane put her arm around Emory. "Come on, you, let's go tear up the mall now."

***

"Mom, this dough is just not kneading right. Look at it. Its consistency is way off."

"Eva, it's fine. Just put a little more water in it, and if it gets too thin, add more flour until you get the right texture."

Eva followed her mom's instructions and was not surprised that they solved her problem. The greatly improved balance made the kneading easy.

"Mom, you always have the perfect answers to my problems."

"If that were only true, Eva. I can manage the baking issues, but life issues are far more complicated. But I do know who to go to for answers—even delayed and unexpected ones."

"I really miss Rick, Mom."

"I know you do, sweetheart, but it's only been a few weeks. He has a lot of things to work out within himself."

"Do you and Dad hate him? Please be honest."

"No, honey, of course, we do not hate Rick. Every night, we pray God will change Rick's heart to be the husband God intends for him to be."

"Really? Mom, that means so much to me. Do you

think the two of us have a chance together in this marriage?"

Before Josie answered, Emory walked in, door slamming behind her. Hearing Eva's question, she offered her opinion. "Well, I told you all along it wasn't going to last."

Both women turned and stared coolly at her.

"I mean, I don't want to be cruel, but I'm a realist." Emory continued.

"Emory!" Josie shot her a long glare. "You need to be supportive of your sister. We all make decisions that are not the best at times, but you don't just give up when things get hard in a marriage."

Emory shrugged her shoulder and grabbed a cookie. "Okay, I'm sorry. Can I sit in here with you guys for a while?"

Eva gave her a forgiving smile and said, "Sure, you may learn something."

"Doubt it, but the cookies are good."

Josie picked up where they had left off. "Right now, it all depends on the choices Rick makes. God will not force him, and we can't change him. It's up to him, but you need to keep reminding yourself of all of this."

"I know, Mom, and I do remind myself. I've talked to Lori a few times, and she has told me that Rick is seeing her husband every day for counseling. She is not privy to how that goes, but she said Rick's consistency is a very good sign."

"Good start. Maybe you do have a chance." Emory took another bite.

Josie ignored the comment. "That's wonderful, Eva, but it is going to take some time."

"Mom?" Eva's voice was edged with uncertainty.

"What, dear?

"Mom, I need you to stop with the baking and look at me."

Josie drew a deep breath and gave Eva her undivided attention. Emory finished her cookie and brushed the crumbs into her hand.

"Mom, I've been talking to Rick on the phone. He has been talking about doing something I'm not sure is a great idea, but he is not being rash about it. He is just talking it through with me."

"Eva, your dad and I know that the two of you have been talking. We've known for a couple of weeks now."

"Yeah, me too," Emory admitted.

"And you didn't say anything? You didn't try to stop us?"

"Honey, it's not our place to stop you. We talked about it and decided that if we intervened, it would just make everything harder. You are a grown, married woman, and we have to let you be exactly that. We raised you right, and you know the Lord. Please live by his will. If you do that, he will work everything else out for you and for Rick."

"Mom, Rick wants to request a discharge from the army and move back home. It's a big step, and I just don't know if he should. He keeps telling me that he is changing, but he thinks we should go to counseling together. He is willing to walk away from his life there for me, for us."

"That sounds very promising, Eva, but it puts a lot of pressure on you, doesn't it?"

"It really does, but he doesn't understand that part of it. He keeps telling me it is his decision, and he is doing it for both of us. I do truly love him, and I believe that all we need is a second chance."

"Wow, I think I'm just now getting this. That's pretty cool that he would do that. Love sure makes people do crazy things," Emory concluded. *I would do that for Shane. I know I would.*

Josie gave Emory what she perceived to be a why-are-you-even-here look and continued to talk to Eva. *Don't worry, Mom. Shane is coming to get me soon so you can have your precious bonding time with Eva. I want to be out of here as much as you want me to leave.*

"Eva, just take your time. We will support whatever your decision is. We are on your side—yours and Rick's."

"Thank you for saying that, Mom. It makes what I need to ask you a lot easier. I know how you and Dad feel about Rick. I had never seen Dad so mad or you so hurt as when you saw what he had done. Even so, I know how forgiving you both can be, so I need to ask you if you will go with me to see him. Actually, Rick has asked me if you would see him because he wants to apologize to you. He said before he did anything about getting out of the service, he wanted to ask for my forgiveness and yours. So, what do you think?"

"I'm all for it," Emory opined, just to get under her mother's skin.

Eva smiled. "Thanks, Emory; good to have you on my side. Mom?"

Josie thought for a moment before answering, "You know I will have to talk about this with your dad, and you can be sure I will tonight. When do you want to do this?"

"I don't want you to think we are rushing this, but

we need to do it in early December at the latest."

"My goodness, Eva, this is already November. That is pretty short notice."

"I know, but it's the Army that is really setting the timetable. If he gets a discharge, they want him out before the end of the year. I don't know why; something to do with end-of-year manpower numbers. Anyway, that is what is driving this along so quickly."

A horn beeped outside, and Emory stood up. "That's Shane. We were on the way to the mall, but she had to run an errand. So to the mall we go. I'll be back before dinner."

"Have fun, Emory," Eva said as the door slammed.

Emory jumped into the passenger seat while Shane threw a couple of gym bags in the trunk. Shane wheeled around, took two strides, and jumped behind the steering wheel.

Shane backed out of the driveway and drove quickly to the mall, chatting with Emory the entire way. They found a great parking place, and Shane pulled in singing with the radio. In her busyness, she didn't notice what Emory had found in her console. Panic flooded her when she realized she had been found out by her best friend.

"Shane? Please don't tell me this is what I think it is."

Emory held up a baggie with two hand-rolled smokes in it. She held her breath, hoping she was wrong but knowing she was not.

"Emory, put that down, especially here. Don't let anyone see it."

"Then it is ....?

"Yes, Emory, it's pot." Shane put her head down

and searched for a way to explain. Finally, she spoke again. Shaken and emotional, the words did not come easily.

"Look, Emory, I could lie to you and tell you I was holding it for someone else, but I just can't be dishonest with you. I told you when we first started hanging out that I'm not good like you. I don't even really know why you want to be around me. I'm not good for you."

"Shane, what are you talking about? You are my best friend, the best friend I have ever had. I thought we shared everything with each other. But this is a pretty big secret you have been hiding."

"I know, I know, but I was afraid of what you would think. This was an accident. It should not have been in my car. I had promised myself I would never have it with me when I was with you. Please don't be mad at me, Em; I just made a mistake."

"If that is the way you felt, why didn't you just stop smoking the stuff, not just for me, but for you, too? Do you know how much trouble you can get into if they find you with this?"

Shane began shaking her head and grew defensive. "No, Emory, not you, too. I don't need any lectures from you. We have always done your things like going to the Teen Center, working with kids, and all that stuff. But as much as I like you, you have no right to tell me who I should be and how I should act. I'm a big girl, and I've been through more than you have even dreamed about. Don't think you can just say stop it, and I will jump. If that's the way you see our friendship, that's awfully selfish."

Emory was stunned by the outburst. Her stomach in knots. She felt a strange urge to cry and lash out at Shane at the same time. A powerful sense of anger and hurt gripped her heart, and she grappled with a response. Finally, the emotion spilled out. "Shane, how could you say such hateful words to me. I have bent over backwards to make you feel like you belong at school, at my home, everywhere. You are the one who has no right to speak to me like that."

"Oh yeah, you have done so much for me. Poor Shane. Where would I be without the great Emory, the all-American girl? Give me a break. I've been carting your butt around in my car ever since I came to this crummy town. You are the most immature moocher I've ever known."

Emory threw the baggie at Shane, got out, and slammed the door. "Fine, Shane, I'll never ask you to give me a ride again. In fact, I'll never ask you to do anything with me again!"

"That's fine with me, you little punk!"

"Shut up and go smoke your precious weed."

"Exactly what I plan to do. You have no idea what a relief it is to be free of you and all of your goody, goody ways. What was I ever thinking being friends with you?"

Shane started the car, put it in gear, and pushed the gas pedal hard. The squealing tires caught the attention of all the bystanders. Emory stood alone in the parking lot, numb from what had just happened. She had no idea what all the emotions inside her meant, and the worst of it was she had no one to talk to about it—except Pepper, the one who always listened.

Chapter 14
Despair & Desire

The journal lay open in her lap, best buddy Pepper at her side. Emory read through her entries over the last three weeks. The words were raw. Reading them felt like someone was continuously plunging daggers into her heart. She looked at the first entry after her fight with Shane.

Why do I miss you so much, Shane? Why am I so alone and afraid to just go on with my life? I don't even know what happened with us; I would never try to change you. I want to pick up the phone, but I'm scared—scared you will make this separation permanent.

Flipping through several pages, she came to the entry from a few days earlier.

They say time is supposed to heal all wounds. They could not be more wrong. The longer I am away from you, the more it hurts. Why won't you call me? Why won't you even look at me at school? Shane, I want you back, but you will not even pick up your phone when I call. Now with Thanksgiving break, I can't even see you. This cannot go on much longer. I can't take it.

A knock at her bedroom door brought her head up. *Shane? Did she come to see her?* Hope filled her as she jumped to the door.

"Oh, hi, Mom."

"That's a nice greeting. Emory. Your dad and I have something we need to talk to you about to see if you are okay with it. Can you come downstairs?"

"Sure, Mom. Right now?'

"Yes, if you don't mind."

When Emory walked into the living room, her dad and Eva were already there. It appeared to be a Johnson family meeting time. They had not had one of these in quite a while, at least not one where Emory was invited. What could this possibly be about? Her disinterest gave way to unexpected fear. Was it about Shane? Had they found out about her drug use? At an even deeper level that she did not want to admit to herself, she feared they had found out about how Emory felt toward Shane.

Nervous and panicked, Emory asked, "What's going on here?"

Lee took control as he always did at their family meetings. He motioned for Emory to take a seat. He put his arm around Josie.

"Emory, we need to discuss something with you because you are the only one that has been left out of the loop."

Oh no, here it comes. They do know, and they are going to send me to some kind of counselor or away to a private school. She grabbed for Pepper and held him close, braced for what was to come.

"Dad, just say it."

"Emory, relax, it's not bad; in fact, we hope it is the beginning of something really good. Eva and Rick are trying to work things out, and we are trying to help them all we can. Since we just finished celebrating Thanksgiving yesterday, we thought now would be the best time to do that. You are out of school, and everything is pretty much shut down until next Monday, so we are planning to take Eva to see Rick tomorrow. Honey, I'm sorry to spring this on you at the last minute, but it just kind of fell into place today."

Emory's relief was short-lived. Emotions raced through her again. Her mind was filled with thoughts of envy and jealousy. The internal voices would not be quiet. *Sure, go take care of your precious Eva, the daughter you really love. Don't give another thought about me. Have you no clue what I am going through? What about my breakup? None of you have even asked me about Shane. She hasn't been around for weeks, and it doesn't matter to you at all. Go ahead. I'm fine without you. Go patch up Eva's problems as always.*

"Emory, did you hear what your dad just said? Josie interrupted. "Honey, we will be gone overnight, so we were wondering if you wanted to invite Shane to stay with you. We don't feel comfortable leaving you by yourself. We will call you as soon as we get there and again when we are getting ready to come home."

Emory stared in disbelief at her mom and dad. *If you only knew what you were saying! Well, no matter, I am old enough to be on my own regardless of what you guys think of me. I am already dealing with a lot more than you know—on my own at that. Shane was right. Maybe I'm just a coddled kid because that is the way I've always been treated. I wonder why you two even bothered to have me. Oh, that's right, you were trying for a boy. Well, maybe that's what you got and don't even know it. All right, I'll let you off the hook. A little lie will please you.*

Emory smiled, "Mom, Dad, don't worry about a

thing. I'm sure Shane would love to come over and stay. You go do what you need to do, and everything here will be fine. Your timing couldn't be better, really. Shane was just asking me when we were going to get together again."

"Good, then it's settled. We will get packed tonight. Girls, I'm pulling out at seven a.m. whether or not you have your makeup on."

Josie and Eva laughed while Emory, feeling lonelier than she ever thought possible, stared into Pepper's big brown eyes. She stood up and walked invisibly toward the stairs, leaving the sounds of happy laughter behind her. Stopping at the first step, she pivoted and gazed at the phone.

Muttering to herself, "I've got plenty of time to waste. I'll try one more time. Might as well finish playing out this charade to keep the folks happy." After the sixth ring with no answer, she hung up. Neither disappointed nor surprised, she headed toward the stairs. Stopping short, she yelled into the living room, "All set, Mom. Shane will be over tomorrow around nine," she lied again, realizing she was getting good at it.

"Okay, honey, I know how much Shane likes my spaghetti. There will be leftovers, and Eva and I just baked some fresh cookies."

"That's great. Thanks. Come on, Pepper, let's go."

***

Shane took another hit on the joint and sang with the music. Staying high had been her remedy when her mom left her, and she depended on it to do the same again. Yet, it seemed to fall short of its intended purpose. Kicking the basketball across her bedroom, she looked at it with love and hate. Basketball was Emory, and Emory was too good for her. She could never be friends with someone like her. The girl lived in a bubble with rules and beliefs that were like chains to Shane.

She talked to the ball. "Dear sweet, Emory, I am doing you a great favor staying away from you. Shoot, Shane, who are you kidding? This is killing you, and you are too much of a coward to admit it. You're too afraid to tell Emory you are sorry, and you want to start all over again. Man, I miss you, Emory. I miss you so much." Taking another hit, Shane breathed in the smoke as deeply as she could and held her breath, allowing the smoke to stay in her system for maximum effect. Reaching up to the radio, she turned the music up louder, but nothing seemed to drown out the despairing cries in her heart. Switching to her favorite cassette, she put on the headphones, closing her eyes to shut out the world. She didn't hear the phone ring.

Chapter 15
Funeral for a Friend

*E*mory lay in bed after a fitful night. She couldn't remember if she ever fell asleep, only that she had wept until she had no more tears. It had not been her plan to get up and see the family off, but she couldn't sleep anyway. The clock read six-thirty; they should be getting ready to load up. Struggling with whether to lie there or go downstairs, another surge of grief rumbled through her.

Looking out her window, she could see the twinkling stars and an almost full moon. The sight triggered thoughts of a night when she was eleven years old, and her mother was with her talking to her about God and how much he loved her and the world. He loved her so much he sent his Son to die on the cross for her sins. Because she accepted Jesus into her heart that night, she still believed her eternity would be with Him. Yet, that assurance did nothing to heal her broken heart right now.

Rubbing her tired eyes, she rolled over and looked at the picture of Shane and her on the nightstand. That was the day they had hiked to the crest of the mountain and celebrated their achievement with milkshakes afterward. One of the guys at the malt shop had snapped the picture for them, and Shane had developed it herself. She even matted it and put it in a handmade frame. As evidenced by the picture and a half dozen sketches that decorated her room, Shane was gifted. There was the first sketch of Emory and Pepper. It was still her favorite.

Rolling back over, she slid her hand down Pepper's furry back and sighed. Finally, she decided to do what her parents had always told her to do, she talked to God.

"God, it's me, Emory. A long time ago, I became one of yours. Father, I still believe you love me, but I don't understand why you are doing this to me. You teach us in the Bible to obey your commands, and then you give me feelings that are exactly the opposite of what you command. You cannot be so cruel as to do this on purpose. What have I done wrong? Why have you made me this way? Why did you bring Shane to me and then snatch her away? It's not fair. God, you're not fair. Do you hear me? I'm begging you to stop these feelings. I want to go back to just being me, but I don't even know who I am anymore."

Frustrated, Emory pounded the pillow with her fist. Pepper jumped and whimpered. Throwing back the covers, she rolled out of bed, put on her house shoes, and headed down the stairs to the familiar voices of her family. Josie went back over the snacks she had packed as Lee picked up the suitcases to take outside. Eva was at the table drinking coffee and trying to wake up.

"Oh, hey, Emory," Eva muttered. "Didn't think you would be up this early on Saturday."

Josie stopped her task and looked at Emory, "Honey, you didn't have to get up. Hope we didn't wake you."

"Good morning to you, too, Mom. You guys better hurry. Can't be late, you know."

Emory waited to see if either of them caught the sarcasm in her voice. As expected, they missed it. She shuffled over to the refrigerator, discovered they were out of orange juice, and chose milk instead.

"Well, it's good you are up because I wanted to remind you that we are trusting you and Shane to be on your best behavior. I expect this house to look as good when we get home as it does now. I hope you and Shane have a good time, but your curfew is still intact. Be home with doors locked no later than ten. There is plenty of food, and you are welcome to it. I left you a little money, too, in case you want to catch a movie or something. I think that's all. Do you have any questions?"

"Yeah, Mom, when are you going to switch off the drill sergeant bit and get in the car?"

"All right, all right. I just wanted to make sure you had everything you need. Come on, Eva, your dad is in the driver's seat, and he is one punctual guy. Bye Emory, love you."

"Goodbye, Mom."

The door closed like a prison cell. Emory carried the milk back to the refrigerator and put it on the shelf. Her stomach refused to take anything.

Do you, Mom? Do you love me? You show your love about the same way God does. Neither of you even knows me or anything I am going through. How can you possibly think I believe you love me?

Pounding the wall, she screamed as loudly as she could. Wailing, she lowered herself down the wall to the cold linoleum floor. *I just want to die! I have no one, and no one would miss me.*

Crossing her arms over her propped-up knees, she cried dry tears of anguish. It was only when Pepper came over and licked her face that she looked up. She sat there with Pepper, hurting until a numbness of her soul enveloped her.

It was ten o'clock when she finally got dressed and headed outside with Pepper to hike the pastureland. They had walked these grounds together more times than she could remember. Just across the street was an area of wide-open space. They walked until they had reached the top of the hill that overlooked the town on the other side and looked at the single elm tree growing there as alone as she felt. The cool November air was tempered by the sun. This was her favorite time of year, and while many leaves had already fallen, it was still quite beautiful. She breathed in deeply and slowed her pace as she could tell that Pepper was laboring just a little bit. He would follow her to the ends of the earth on his last leg if he had to. She knew that without a doubt.

Stopping, the two sat together in the tall grass and looked at the cloudless sky. This day and this hike would normally fill her heart with overwhelming joy, but today, nothing—nothing but anger and loss and loneliness. They stayed for only a while, drinking in the best nature had to give but finding no refreshment.

"Come on, boy, let's head back. It's a long walk. Just because I can't eat doesn't mean that you can't."

They retraced their path even more slowly than before. It was a little easier going down the sloping incline, and Pepper seemed to be doing a lot better. Approaching the road, they only had a few more yards to the house. Yes, he was going to make it. Looking down and encouraging Pepper, Emory never saw the speeding car until it was too late. With one foot on the road and Pepper slightly ahead, she saw only chrome and then heard the bone-crunching sound of the impact.

"Pepper!" she screamed, and then everything went black.

***

Shane sat up in bed and looked around her room. The sun streaming through the blinds illuminated a mess of clothes and albums strewn haphazardly across the floor and chair. She flinched from the bright light and let out a mild cuss word. Her wall clock showed nine forty-five already. No matter, she might just spend the whole day in bed.

Her midnight, munchie-induced snacks told her otherwise. Grudgingly, she got up and went into the bathroom. Disgusted with herself, she looked in the mirror and was horrified at what she saw. Three weeks had aged her three years.

Going to the bed, she sat on it, trying to find some form of orientation for her life. She looked at the copy of the picture she had given Emory. The two of them at the malt shop, arms thrown over each other's shoulder. Happy together, taking life in and enjoying every minute of it. What had happened to them?

Emory, I am so sorry. I miss you. Shane, get ahold of yourself. Go into the kitchen and live the rest of your life. You got along fine before Emory. Now get to it.

Throwing on a pair of jeans and a sweatshirt, she walked through the small house to the kitchen. Maybe she could share breakfast with her dad. She loved him, and he tried to love her, but those words were

117

never spoken. After they had been abandoned, he was empty, no longer possessing the capacity to love fully. He did the best he could for Shane, and they each coped in their own way. He knew she smoked; she knew he drank heavily. Still, there was a strange sort of respect each for the other. He would provide all she needed as best he could afford, but he was only a shell of a man now.

She reached a vacant kitchen and saw a note on the table. Printed in large block letters, by an obviously shaking hand, she recognized her dad's imprint right away. A man of few words, the note simply read, "Baby, gone to car show with Miles. Back tonight. Dad."

She tossed the note back on the table, glad that her dad was getting out but knowing tonight probably meant a drunken return. She understood his pain more now than ever before. Sticking her hands in her pocket, she felt the joint she had forgotten. Looking at it, she felt as hollow as she knew her dad was and shoved it back in.

Shane, what is wrong with you? I can't take this anymore.

I've got to talk to her. I'll just call and tell her I'm sorry, and that will be all. Short and to the point. I'll just hear her voice and know that she is okay. Then I will just say that I did not mean any of those cruel things I said to her.

Simultaneous chills and sweat seized her entire body. Edging closer to the phone, she reached out and picked up the receiver. She dialed and held her breath. Each ring brought her closer to hyperventilation. After ring five, the answering machine kicked in. It was Emory's voice, "Hello, you have reached the

Johnsons' house. We are sorry we can't take your call right now but let us know who you are, and we promise to call you back soon. Have a blessed day."

Shane slammed the phone down. Just hearing Emory's voice rocked her to the core. Shaken but determined, Shane knew exactly what she had to do, and nothing was going to stop her from seeing the only source of love she had ever known.

The fifteen-minute drive to Emory's house felt like an eternity. Driving too fast for the narrow roads, she skidded twice on wet leaves and blew by every stop sign. She could have made this drive blindfolded. She had driven it so many hundreds of times—so many times, laughing and singing with Emory. Memories crowded her mind; longing propelled her heart.

Drawing closer to the house, fear crept in. Emory was right around the next curve. *Should I just slow down and drive on by or stop and knock on the door? What would Emory's parents think? What if she isn't there? What if she is and refuses to see me? How would Emory react? Does she hate me?*

Pushing the fear aside, she drove on. Steering the car around the curve, Emory's house came in sight. Her heart accelerated as the car slowed. She was just about to make the left turn into the long driveway when she saw them—two large heaps on the side of the road. Recognition came when she spotted Emory's distinct maroon and white school jacket.

"Emory!"

Slamming on the brakes, Shane didn't even bother getting the car out of the road. She flung open the door and ran to where Emory and Pepper lay side by side. Pepper's lifeless body was the first thing she saw.

"Emory, Emory. No, please God, no, no!"

She fell to her knees and brushed the hair from Emory's eyes. A large knot protruded from her forehead. Her face was scratched all over, but none of the cuts seemed to be deep.

Emory groaned and moved her head, then opened her eyes. Shane breathed a prayer of a thousand thank you'd and stroked Emory's face.

"Emory, thank God, you are alive. Are you okay? Don't move. I got you, Emory. You are going to be okay."

Emory slowly became conscious of her surroundings. She blinked her eyes twice before realizing it really was Shane leaning over her. "Shane? Shane! It really is you."

"It's me, Emory, I'm back, and I am here to take care of you."

The joy was short-lived as Emory's memory returned. "Pepper! Where's Pepper? The car hit him. Where is he, Shane?"

Shane blocked Emory from seeing the heartbreaking body of her beloved dog. It was not something Shane ever wanted Emory to have to see, yet she knew it was inevitable. She swallowed hard and, with chin quivering, tried to break the news. Before she could get the first word out, Emory struggled and sat up. Shane grabbed hold of her and pulled her in tightly to her body. Looking over Shane's shoulder, she saw Pepper.

"I'm so sorry, Emory. I'm so sorry."

Emory's body convulsed in uncontrolled waves of anguish and grief. Eyes closed, she wailed in agony. "Pepper! My Pepper! Noooooooooo, Pepper, you can't be gone!"

Shane rocked her back and forth and tried to calm her. There was no consoling Emory, but she would try.

"Listen to me, sweetheart. Pepper lived a long and very good life with you. He left this world doing the thing he loved most, walking with you by his side. He felt no pain. It happened in an instant. You will see him again over the rainbow bridge. I really believe that."

Emory continued to sob into Shane's chest. Her mind and emotions fully engulfed with the kind of grief that only can come with pure love.

"Emory, I know how much it hurts. But you have to listen to me right now; I have to look at you and make sure you are not injured. I need to take you to the emergency room."

"No, no, Shane. We have to take care of Pepper first. We have to take care of him first."

Shane knew there would be no way to talk Emory out of her determination. Against her better judgments, she agreed.

"Okay, babe, I have a blanket in the back of my car. I want to help you stand up and walk to the car with me. I'm going to put you in the back seat. Then I will wrap Pepper in the blanket and bring him to you. Do you think you can walk?"

"Help me up, Shane. I think I can."

Shane slowly began to lift her up but noticed Emory wince when she touched her shoulder. "You must have landed on that shoulder. Come on, girl, let's get you to the car."

Gingerly, Emory lowered herself into the back seat and watched Shane wrap Pepper with the tenderness he deserved. Shane lifted the precious bundle and carried him to her, laying him in her lap.

"Thank you, Shane. Thank you."

Shane tried to smile and asked, "Where do you want to lay him to rest?"'

"Up there, Shane. At the top of the hill. I can look out my window and see him from there."

Pulling the car around, they drove down the driveway. Shane got out and took a pick and shovel from Lee's tool shed. She steered the car around and drove across the road and through the pasture until they reached the top of the hill.

The ground was hard from lack of rain, so it took Shane a while to dig the hole deep enough for Pepper. Emory watched from the car, still holding Pepper, still trying to find her footing in reality.

Shane tossed the shovel to the side and walked over to the car. Wordlessly, she lifted Pepper out of Emory's arms and carried him to the grave. She placed him into the ground that he had run upon as a pup, that he had struggled to walk upon just a few moments ago.

Shane came back to the car and helped Emory get out and walk to the site. She knew Emory was in shock, so she tried to be there for her in all ways possible.

Emory stared down at the blanket, "Goodbye, my friend. You were the best. You were the best. I pray God will let me be with you in heaven one day. I bet he will have some great hills for us to climb together."

Sobbing again, she turned to Shane and buried her head into her chest. "Shane, please take care of him."

"I will, honey."

Guiding her back to the car, Shane quickly returned and shoveled the dirt back over the beloved dog—the one who would never be forgotten or rivaled. "Goodbye, old friend. You will truly be missed," Shane's tears streamed down her face.

"Shane!"

She looked up and saw Emory getting out of the car. Wobbling and unsteady, Emory was motioning to her. She ran to her and caught her as she passed out.

Chapter 16
The Crossing

*T*he day had been about as perfect as anyone could have expected for traveling. Light traffic and great weather still did not lessen the anxiety. Arriving at three o'clock in the afternoon allowed them time to check into the hotel room before meeting with Rick. They freshened up and talked about keeping all expectations in check.

Eva anxiously paced the floor. Though they had been talking on the phone, it wasn't the same as seeing him in person. "I'm so nervous, Mom. Why am I so worked up about this?"

"Eva, I know you are. It's understandable. Wherever your heart is, there will be these feelings. But do not let fear get in your way. Besides, honey, we are here for you."

"I know you are, Mom, and I can't tell you how much it means to me that you are both here. I know you will never let me down. I just hope one day I can have that same assurance with Rick."

Lee returned with a full bucket of ice. He walked in and smiled at his two girls, trying to hide the turmoil going on within him, too. This was a pivotal point in his daughter's life. Rick had been saying all the right things but what he had done was indefensible. He wondered if Rick knew how much he had wanted to beat the living daylights out of him when he first saw Eva's black eyes. But that was then. Now they all had been praying for Rick to be a changed man. That was the only way reconciliation was going to be possible.

"Looks like it's getting close to five. Are we ready?"

"Yes, Dad."

"Josie, are you ready?"

"Yes, but I just need to make a quick call home to Emory." Josie picked up the receiver and dialed. The phone rang until the answering machine kicked in. She smiled at hearing Emory's sweet voice but hung up without leaving a message.

"Guess she and Shane are out. I'll call her back later."

***

The emergency room was jammed with people. Emory had regained consciousness, but she was still groggy. The waiting was brutal. Shane had looked at the clock when they first arrived at around noon. Other than filling out paperwork, she had been staring at it ever since. She wanted more than anything to know that Emory was okay and to take her home.

After two hours, they finally took Emory back to a small, private room for another half-hour wait. Eventually, the doctor came in and examined her and ordered x-rays of her head and shoulder. Shane lied and said that they were sisters so she could stay. She also told them about the hit and run, which required more paperwork.

Emory said very little, but she insisted Shane stay close to her. Her eyes were vacant, yet she knew she was not alone. Even with Pepper gone, Shane was there. Shane was back in her life.

The doctor came in and told the girls the good news, "Fortunately, all the x-rays have come back negative. Your shoulder was bruised and knocked out of the socket, but physical therapy should resolve it. Young lady, you are a medical marvel. It is incredible to me that your head injury did not cause any internal bleeding or swelling. Given the report of the accident, I am perplexed by these results. I would have laid odds that we were going to have to do surgery to relieve pressure on the brain. You must have quite the guardian angel watching over you."

Shane was elated, "Thanks, Doctor, thank you so much for everything. Do you think I can take her home now?"

"Yes, you may. Emory, I am giving you some pain medication but take it only as needed. Get some rest. That's what you need more than anything."

Twenty minutes later, Emory and Shane entered the Johnsons' house. The phone was ringing as they made it to the couch.

"Let it ring, Shane. It's my mom, and I can't deal with her right now. She'll call back later. When she calls back, I don't want her to know what has happened until they get home. I just can't take the hysteria."

"Okay, Emory."

"You know they think you are spending the night with me."

"They would be right. I am not leaving your side, not ever again. Emory, I drove over here earlier to tell you I'm sorry for all the things I said to you. I miss you, and I just can't stand this fighting. You know I did not mean any of those things."

"Shane, I'm sorry, too—so, so sorry. I've been miserable without you. I have tried to call, but you never answered."

"I know. I'm ashamed of myself for being such a fool and so darned stubborn. I kept lying to myself about how I didn't need you to live my life. Truth is, I do need you more than I have ever needed anyone."

Shane hesitated, then continued, "So I finally came to my senses and called you this morning. When you didn't answer, I heard your voice on the machine. That broke me, Emory. I came as fast as I could get here."

"If you had not been here for me, Shane, I don't know what I would have done. You are the only one who has ever been there for me. I can't tell you how much what you did for Pepper meant to me. I watched how kind and gentle you were with him. You loved him, too, didn't you, Shane?"

'Yes, I really did love him, Emory. Anyone that can make you so happy makes me happy, too. I'm going to make a really nice headstone for his grave, so when you look up on that hill, you will be able to see the marker really well."

"Oh, Shane, I know it will be beautiful. You always create such wonderful things." Another wave of emotion swept over Emory. Her body started to shake with overwhelming grief. Shane reached out and pulled her to her side. She put an arm around her as they lay back on the couch together.

"It's all right, Emory. I got you. Emory?"

"Yes?"

"Emory, I, I uh, I lo... love you," Shane whispered.

Emory felt a stirring in her core she had never known existed. She had been told a thousand times before by her parents that she was loved but never,

ever like this. This was so inexpressibly real. Shane had said to her exactly what she, too, had been feeling but was too afraid to say out loud. But now that Shane had opened the door, the fear was gone.

She pulled away slightly to look into Shane's eyes, "I love you, too, Shane."

Shane smiled and leaned toward Emory. "I want to give you something—something so that even when we are not together, a part of me will be there wherever you are." She took off her class ring and picked up Emory's hand. Sliding it on her finger, her smile broadened, and both realized then what they were truly exchanging.

Collapsing back into Shane, Emory breathed in deeply. She felt so safe, so good with those arms around her. Foreign as all of this was, it felt utterly right to her at that moment. Her eyes grew heavy as they lay there together listening to the radio playing one of her favorite songs. Dr. Hook sang, *"Oh, oh, sharing the night together."*

***

Rick was already there when the Johnsons arrived at the restaurant. They walked in, observing its beautiful decor. Eva knew it well. It was a local favorite but a little too upscale for her husband's salary. It did not take long for her to spot him. Tall and tanned, his muscular build was evident even through his dress coat. He looked good, like the man she gave her heart to in marriage.

Rick rose as they approached the table. He looked long at Eva, then greeted Lee and Josie. His face and his voice clearly showed how nervous he was.

"Hello, Mr. and Mrs. Johnson. I can't tell you how

much I appreciate your agreeing to meet with me. Please sit down."

Lee's face was stern and difficult to read, but he thanked Rick and helped Josie with her chair.

Rick turned to Eva and half smiled, "Hi, Eva, thank you for coming. You look really good; I've missed you."

Eva felt unnerved and afraid to speak, so she simply nodded and sat down as Rick pulled the chair out for her.

Rick fidgeted in his chair before he spoke the words he had been playing in his mind since the day Eva left him. "I want to begin by apologizing to you, Eva. I am sorry for the way I treated you. You deserve better. I make no excuses; I was wrong, and I am ashamed of the way I acted. I want to ask you to forgive me and take me back as your husband."

He turned and looked directly at Lee and Josie. "Sir, Ma'am, I am deeply sorry for the way I treated Eva, and I am appalled at my own actions. No man should ever raise a hand to a woman in any circumstance. I promise you that I will never, ever do anything like that again. I love your daughter with all my heart and will spend my life protecting her and providing for her. I ask you to accept my apology, and I ask for a second chance to be a good husband for Eva."

Eva broke the silence, "I love you, Rick, and I want us to work all of this out and to be together again for the rest of our lives."

Lee followed Eva, speaking with authority but kindness. "Rick, you have broken a trust—a trust with us but, more importantly, with Eva and with God. You know that words are nice, but they are never enough. You are going to have to earn that trust back again from all of us."

"Yes, sir, I know you are right. That is why I have been getting counseling from the chaplain, and I have rededicated myself to the Lord. I know I need his divine help to be the husband Eva deserves. It will take time, but I am committed to honoring our wedding vows."

Josie spoke this time, "Rick, as I have told Eva, we are on your side. Lee and I want you two to make this marriage a lasting commitment. But Eva is more precious to us than our own lives. We have to know in our hearts you will love her above even yourself."

"Mrs. Johnson, I'm willing to do anything to prove just that. If you will allow Eva to stay here with me until Christmas, I will work every day to show her and you that I am a man of my word. I have spoken to the chaplain, and he and his wife, Lori, have agreed to allow Eva to stay with them at night just as an added precaution to ease your fears. We will have time to get to know each other all over again, almost as if we are dating again. If all of this meets your approval, I will be forever grateful to you."

"What about you, Eva? What do you think?" Lee asked.

"Well, Dad, Rick had already told me what he was planning to say to you. We feel like it would be best for us to get to know each other again slowly."

Lee and Josie exchanged looks, and Josie spoke, "Lee, we both really thought highly of Lori when we met her."

Lee nodded and turned to Rick and Eva. "Rick, you have spoken well for yourself tonight. Our God is a God of second chances. If we learn from our mistakes, we all become better for them. I am confident I speak for Josie as well when I tell you that, yes, we do forgive you. But I want you to know, son, that it is only by the grace of God that we can do so. It is more painful than I hope you will ever know for a father to see his daughter hurt in any way. This is just the first step, but it is a really big one."

"Sir, I can only imagine what you thought of me, and I cannot tell you how many times I have wanted to take it all back. But I do understand what you are saying, and I believe God wants this for us. I have received his forgiveness and now yours. I hope to get it from Eva as well, but we will need this time together to make that happen."

"I agree with you on that, and you have my approval for Eva to stay as long as Josie is okay with it."

Josie smiled and reached for Eva's hand, "Daughter, you guard your heart and always trust in the Lord. We will miss you so much, but our love is with you always."

"Thanks, Mom, Dad. And can I tell them the rest, Rick?"

"Sure, sweetheart."

"We decided that if you approved of all of this, Rick would go ahead with his discharge request. He has been saving all of his leave so that we will be home for good three days before Christmas."

Lee's practical mind kicked in. "That's wonderful, honey, but what then? Neither of you has a job. How will you live?"

"That is a very good question, Mr. Johnson. I'm a pretty skilled mechanic, and I think I can get a decent job to start, but one day I want to own my own shop."

"Yeah, Dad, we know it will be tight at first, but it always has been for us. I can work part-time and go to school, and Rick's dad has an apartment we can use rent-free until we get on our feet."

"It will be tough sledding at first, but you kids seem to have your eyes wide open. We will give you any support we can."

"Excuse me, sir, have you had enough time to select your order yet?" The waiter stood next to Lee, pen and pad in hand.

Lee laughed, "My good man, I think we all want the same thing, but give us a few more minutes to look over the menu.

Chapter 17
Conflicted

1982, 17-years-old

"Come on, Emory, quit loafing. What in the world is wrong with you? Oh, come on! I've seen six-year-olds play better defense than that. You are twice as fast as Mara, and she blew right by you! What are you doing?"

Frustrated, Coach Radcliff blew his whistle. "Okay, I've seen enough. Everybody on the line. We are going to do some wind sprints in honor of Emory's half-hearted efforts today. And you, Shane, you are just as bad as Emory. I don't know where either one of your minds are, but they are not on basketball. You two get to stand over here with me and watch your teammates suffer for your lack of effort."

"Coach, that's not fair," Mara and the rest of the team grumbled.

"You're right. It is not fair. I wanted to make a point to these two that when they put themselves before the team, everyone suffers. Okay, everyone to the showers. Emory, you and Shane come to my office. Now!"

Stone-faced, the three made their way across the gym and down the corridor.

Coach Radcliff sat down behind his desk and motioned for the girls to sit on the opposite side. He looked down at some statistics. Leaning forward, he placed both hands on his desk as if to compose himself.

"It is with the greatest of restraint that I'm not yelling loud enough for the coach at the next school to hear me. I don't know what has gotten into you two. Whatever is going on with you has got to stop and stop now. For two teammates who are supposed to be best friends, I've never seen such outright animosity."

He fixed his gaze on Emory, "And you, the team captain, are letting us all down more than anyone. I know you were named to the all-state team last year, but that was then. This year you couldn't make the pick-up team. I can't even tell you how painful it is for me to watch you lose your passion for the game. You possess all the skills to get a scholarship to a big-name school. Big strides are being made in women's sports, and you could be a part of it. Please don't throw that away."

He pounded his fist on his clipboard, "I'm going to give it to you flat out: either decide you are going to give your full effort to this team or don't show up tomorrow. I mean it, Emory. It's not fair to the other girls when you are playing like this. You decide between now and tomorrow what it's going to be."

Not giving her a chance to reply, the coach turned to address Shane. He cleared his throat and shifted in his chair. "Same goes for you, Shane. You are a senior, and you need to be a leader for the younger players. Get your mind in the game or go do whatever it is you are thinking about."

"Look, girls, this team needs both of you if we are going to have a chance at taking the state title. I can't do this part of the game for you. We need your hearts and your minds to work together toward our common goal. I know I am being harsh, but we are a make-or-break point, and I will do everything I can to see that this team plays to its highest potential."

He sat back in his chair again and looked sky-ward, then back at the girls. Neither of his players had moved. He studied them, acknowledging that he would never in a thousand lifetimes understand teenage girls, but he loved to coach them.

"Have I been clear to you?"

"Yes, Coach," they responded in unison.

"Good, do either of you have any questions? I want to make sure we are all on the same page here."

Emory looked at Shane and then at Coach Rad-cliff. "Coach," she said, "I just want to say we are sorry. The team does deserve better than what we have been giving. We will both be here tomorrow, ready to play."

Shane nodded her head in agreement and added, "We want that gold ball this year."

He half smiled, "Proof is in the pudding, girls. Go do your homework or something. I will see you to-morrow, and I expect the best practice we have ever had."

Fifteen minutes later, the girls walked out of the gym to the parking lot. They had not spoken to each other since they left the coach.

"Emory, this is getting ridiculous. Do you want to tell me why you are so mad at me? Look, whatever it is this time, I'm sorry,"

"If you really don't know, that tells me a lot about how much you care about me."

"Oh my gosh, Em, I don't have a clue what you are

talking about. Just tell me so we can get this cleared up, will you?"

Emory whirled around and looked squarely at Shane. "Sure, I'll spell it out to you. I'll make it as clear as day. If you would rather spend time with your senior class buddies than this lowly junior, that's fine by me. And especially that cheerleader Audrey, why do you even give her the time of day? I mean, she is so stuck on herself—exactly the kind of stuff you hate. But she is popular and a pretty."

"Emory, for Pete's sake, will you get a grip on reality? The senior class had a required school function. I didn't want to go to that stupid picnic. Audrey was paired with me to do our fitness evaluations. I don't even like being around her. I swear, you come up with the craziest ideas sometimes."

Emory softened a little but still bristled. "All I know is that you kept me waiting for you for over an hour at the mall. I was depending on you to come and help me pick out something for Eva, but you were off who knows where. Then when I was sitting there like an idiot, a kid came by and said he had just seen you hanging out with Audrey and a bunch of seniors and that you were having a good time and had them all laughing at your jokes. You tell me what I was supposed to think."

"Well, if you had a little bit more trust in me, you would not have left the mall before I got there and explained everything. Instead, I didn't see you until practice, and you act like a jerk. This cold shoulder thing you give me is just plain childish, and so is your unfounded jealousy."

"My, don't you think highly of yourself. Don't even think I am the least bit jealous of you. I just don't care to be stood up and disrespected by you or anyone else."

"You are jealous, and you know it even if you will not admit it. Quit lying to yourself and face it. You know how I feel about you and only you. I would never disrespect you, Emory."

Looking at Shane, she realized that she desperately loved and needed her. For the first time, she began to comprehend that it was her fear of losing Shane that made her feel all of the things that triggered her reactions. Yes, maybe Shane was right.

"Shane, I don't want to fight with you anymore. Maybe there is some truth in what you are saying. I just don't want to ever face life without you."

"And you won't, Emory, but you have to trust me, and I have to trust you. Hearts are easily broken and seldom fully mend when they are. We have to trust each other."

"You are right, Shane. I'm sorry. So, what do we do now?"

"Well, if you are up for it, what do say we pick up a pizza and drive out to the country? We could smoke one of my hand-rolled specialties then pig out as we watch the sunset."

"You had me at pizza, but you captivated me at the sunset."

"Good, let's go make up."

"I'll never refuse an offer like that from you, but you are not off the hook. You still have to go to the mall with me tomorrow and help me pick out a gift."

Shane laughed, "Ugh, okay, my dear, whatever you say."

***

Josie looked at her list to make sure she had not forgotten anything. The party was two days away, and the preparations were far from complete. There would only be finger foods, punch, and, of course, the cake that she would bake herself, this time without Eva.

The kitchen door opened, "Hi, Mom, how is everything coming along?"

She turned and saw her large daughter waddle to a nearby chair. "Eva, what are you doing here? You should be resting."

"Mom, I'm fine, although I do get pretty winded at the slightest exertion."

"No wonder; pregnancy is exhausting, and it can wreak havoc on the body."

"I swear I love the thought of being a mother, but the process is no stroll in the park. I can't believe I still have three months to go. Look at me; I can barely fit through the door."

Josie laughed, "I've been there, Eva. Well, almost there. I never carried twins like you are. I can't wait to be a grandma of two at one time."

"Yeah, when they told Rick and me we were having twins, you should have seen the blood drain from his face. As soon as he recovered, though, he was delirious with excitement. He is going to make a good daddy. You should hear him talk baby talk to my belly."

"I know you two got off to a rough start, but I am so proud of you both. You never gave up on each other, and now God has blessed you for your faithfulness."

"You and Dad played a big part in that, Mom. You supported us the entire time, and I know how hard it was for you to forgive Rick. I thank God every day that both of you gave Rick a second chance. Oh, and that reminds me—oops, can't tell you."

"Eva Jane Johnson Smith, don't do that to me. You have to tell me now. The cat's halfway out of the bag already."

"Okay, since you called me out with my full name, I guess I have no choice. But you can't let on that you know, because Rick wants to be the one to tell you and Dad. His boss promoted him to assistant manager of the shop. It means a three-hundred-dollar a month raise!"

"That's wonderful, Eva, and timely. Your family can use the extra funds with two more mouths to feed."

"Amen."

"So, I do have a question for you while I've got you in the spilling mood."

"What are you trying to pry out of me now? Oh, wait, let me guess. You want to know if we have chosen names."

"So, have you? I know you have! What are they?"

"Yes, we just decided. The boy's name will be Daniel Lee, and the girl's name will be Hannah Josephine."

Josie's eyes teared, and she was speechless.

"Mom, you and Dad have just done so much for us. We wanted to honor you, and we couldn't think of a better way to do it. What do you think? Do you like the names?"

"I love them, and Lee will, too. I still can't believe we are going to be grandparents."

"Better get ready for it. It's really going to happen, and on behalf of my sore feet and cramped bladder, the sooner, the better! Now your turn for secret reveals, please tell me you are making my favorite cake."

"Red velvet with butter crème icing."

"That's the one. That's my cake. What are you making for everyone else?"

Josie laughed and looked at Eva, "Oh, you are serious, aren't you?"

"Almost, but just kidding. I am eating for three, though. Let's not lose sight of that,"

"Oh, I don't think there is any chance that any of us will lose sight of that."

"Mom, don't be mean to the pregnant lady. She needs your compassion and kind help."

"And she shall have it. Now I want you to go lie down and get some rest. I've got a ton of errands to run. Please try to stay until your dad gets home. He would love to see you."

"Okay, I want to see him, too. By the way, where is Emory keeping herself these days? I never see her anymore."

"Oh, she and that friend of hers, Shane, are off somewhere. They are attached at the hip, I think. But something is going on with her. She hasn't been the same since she lost Pepper."

"Well, that was a pretty traumatic loss for her."

"I know. It truly was, but she is just so different. She hardly ever helps out at the Teen Center anymore. She just seems so preoccupied. We hardly see her, and when we do, we never know what her mood is going to be. She swings from really happy to almost hateful. It's just not like her at all."

"Mom, seventeen is a very complicated time in a girl's life. You remember how it was to be caught between being a girl and becoming a young woman."

"Yes, I do remember, but that puzzles me even more. You know she has not once had a serious boyfriend. She has friends that are boys, but they are more like basketball rivals, not the dating kind."

"Might be a blessing, Mom. Maybe she learned something from my impatience and mistakes."

"Maybe. I just hope she will come to us if she is having problems."

"Don't worry, Mom. I'm sure she will work through whatever is going on. I wish we were closer. I really regret how much I teased her when we were younger. But maybe with the twins, it will give us a second chance at being sisters again. I know she loves kids, so I am hoping she will spend more time with me when she visits them."

"I hope so, too, Eva. She could learn a lot from her big sister. Now you go lie down. I'll be back soon."

***

Shane put the last piece of pizza crust in the box, closed it, and tossed it in the car. She walked to the front of the car and jumped on the hood to be next to Emory. Together they lay back onto the windshield and gazed at the sun moving slowly to the other side of the world.

"I love this time of day and sharing it with you, Emory."

"I was just thinking the same thing. Hard to believe that just an hour ago, we were fighting and being dressed down by coach."

"Ah, Coach is wound too tight. As for the fight, I have no idea what you are talking about," Shane smiled.

"Guess you are right. I have forgotten it, too. Oh,

Shane isn't this just so very peaceful—all the colors streaking across the sky like only nature can do? This is God's mighty handiwork on full display."

With those words, a sudden surge of guilt filled her mind. How little time she had spent even thinking about God. Yes, she thanked him every night for her family and for Shane, but she had not really talked with him or listened to him for a very long time.

"Yes, it is beautiful. I need to bring my camera up here and get some shots of you with this backdrop. I can't believe I haven't already done that."

Shane looked at Emory and knew in the long silence something was going on in her head. It was so easy to read her when she was upset, and those mood swings were becoming more frequent.

"Emory, what's wrong?"

Emory remained silent and in deep thought. One of her much-read Bible verses surfaced in her mind from the first chapter of Romans. *"For since the creation of the world God's invisible qualities— his eternal power and divine nature—have been clearly seen, being understood from what has been made so that people are without excuse and no one can be with excuse for not knowing the Lord for he is evident in all of creation."*

Then there was the part of the passage she had read and grappled with for months now: *"For although they knew God, they neither glorified Him as God nor gave thanks to him, but their thinking became futile and their foolish hearts were darkened. Although they claimed to be wise, they became fools and exchanged the glory of the immortal God for images made to look like a mortal human being and birds and animals and reptiles. Therefore, God gave them over in the sinful desires of their hearts to sexual impurity for the de-grading of their bodies with one another. They exchanged the truth about God for a lie and worshiped and served created things rather than the Creator— who is forever praised. Amen. Because of this, God gave them over to shameful lusts. Even their women exchanged natural sexual relations for unnatural ones."*

"Shane, please let's go. Now."

"What? What in the world are you talking about? Why are you acting so squirrelly?"

Emory sat up and jumped off the car. Before she could get the door opened, Shane grabbed her arm.

"We are not going anywhere until you tell me what is going on. You act like you have been bitten by a snake. Here we were enjoying a nice mellow moment together, happy and free, then boom, we got' go. Now you tell me why you are so upset, and we will work it out like we always do. Okay?"

"Shane, please don't make me tell you. I just can't."

"You can't what? You sit here with me and shift mood gears so fast I can't keep up with you. Then you demand we go, no questions asked. Sorry, but you need to let me in on what is going on. Do you know how this makes me feel?"

"That's just it, Shane, I am thinking about how you feel, and this is just not fair to you. It's me. It's my problem, and you can't help me with this."

"Tell me, Emory, is it your guilt again?"

Emory nodded and held her head down. She couldn't look at Shane. "I know I thought I was past all that, but God tells us in the Bible that this is wrong. That we, you and I, are wrong. I love you so much, but I can't turn my back on Jesus. He saved me, and I owe Him my life."

"Emory, am I so bad that he wants you to turn your back on me? Look, neither one of us chose to have these feelings for each other. We were born this way. I have heard those Scriptures you always talk about interpreted in different ways. Some say the real sin the Bible talks about is when straight people decide they want to experiment. It's not a prohibition against those of us he made as we are."

"I'm sorry, Shane. You don't know how many times I've asked God to tell me it's okay, but he will not let me escape the truth. I love you so much, so deeply, but how can I ..."

"Okay, Emory, I'll take you home, but you are going to have to come to terms with this. You can't keep switching on and off like this. I hate it when you do this. I feel like I am corrupting you or something. It's not fair, Emory. You either love me, or you need to let me know you don't."

"Shane, you know I love you, but..."

"There it is again. When you say I love you to anyone, ever, you should never have to follow it with a "but." We could talk about this all night and get nowhere. I'm taking you home, and we will not discuss it anymore today. It just makes me so sick in my heart. I can't deal with it anymore today."

They remained quiet on the ride home. The roller coaster day ended with a plummet that took their breath and their happiness away. As Emory got out of the car, she gazed up the hill at Pepper's grave marker and the shining stars emerging overhead.

Chapter 18
Spoiled Intentions

$\mathscr{L}$ee woke early on Saturday morning and was surprised to find that Josie was already up. He stretched his tight legs in bed and sighed. This getting old thing was for the birds, but it did have its perks. No more getting up in the middle of the night with crying children or changing diapers. Oh, but those were joyful days, and soon his own daughter would know that joy. He sighed again.

"Josie, where are you?"

Josie stepped from the bathroom, already dressed. "Right here, Lee."

"What are you doing up so early? You are even already dressed. What's going on? Something I don't know about?"

"No dear, nothing special. I just woke up early and couldn't go back to sleep, so I decided to get up. I thought I would go down and make you and Emory some banana pancakes."

"Yum! And sausage?"

"And sausage. Yes, my husband, I am doing this for you but for Emory, too. I don't know what in the world is going on with her. She is so moody. She has always been so kind, but lately, she just seems angry. I know something is bothering her."

Lee sat up and shook his head, "I know what you mean. She hardly ever comes by the Teen Center now, and when she does, she might as well not be there. The kids run to her, and she just blows them off. I started to tell her not to bother coming by because it was hurting some of the kids' feelings, but how do I tell my own daughter not to come to the Center?"

"Have you tried to talk to her?" Josie quizzed.

"Not lately. The last time we really tried was the week she came home with her quarterly grade card. She has always gotten straight A's, but this time she had four B's and a C. I don't remember her ever getting a C in her life. It was a pretty substantial change. She just said she had a lot on her mind with basketball and that she had some really hard classes. She promised to do better, and I think she is."

"Yes, I remember that, and we probably should have pushed a little more then. Well, I think the time has come when we are going to have to do something. Everything about her has changed, and I don't feel like we have done anything to help her."

"I'll try to talk to her again. If she will not talk to us, I know some really good Christian counselors who could help her."

"Let's try first. I am not sure she will talk to anyone right now. She seems to have closed herself off from the world. Last week, I heard her hang up on Shane. Now that is seriously not our Emory."

"That's another thing. Shane is not around as much as she used to be. What's up with that?"

"I've been wondering about that myself, but I'm not sure that is a bad thing. I like Shane, but she is getting ready to graduate soon. It's time for Emory to have other friends, or it is going to be a mighty lonely senior year for her."

"Good point. We'll find out what it is somehow. Now weren't you the one that was going to go make us some yummy pancakes?"

"And sausage per the handsome man's request. Will you make sure Emory comes down with you when you are ready?"

"We will be there in about fifteen minutes."

Josie walked down the stairs and stood by the kitchen sink. She looked outside and saw a glorious day just beginning. Filtered sunlight streamed through the window. She pulled back the sheers for an unobstructed view of an early spring day.

"Lord, thank you for getting me up early today to enjoy the beauty you have blessed us with. Thank you for my family, and I ask you to watch over us and protect us. Lord, I make a special plea to you for Emory. We know she is troubled, but we know, too, that she is yours. Provide your wisdom to us as parents on how to help her with whatever her problems are."

Josie took one more look skyward then turned to get the skillet. Before she reached the stove, the phone rang. Puzzled, she walked the length of the kitchen to answer it. Reaching for the phone, her mind fixed on the possibility that it might be Eva. Her heart raced with anticipation.

"Eva?" she answered expectantly.

No answer came back, but someone was definitely on the phone. "Eva? Is that you?"

"No, Mom, it's me, Emory. I need to talk to you and Dad."

***

Emory sat at a table in the diner, staring at her eggs. She only ordered them to be allowed to sit in the diner for a while. No thought was given to eating anything ever again. Last night had been the worst in her life—worse even than when she lost Pepper. Shane called and wanted to meet her. With all the ups and downs they had been through over the last three months, she really did not want to, but Shane had insisted.

She had been sneaking out of the house late at night and riding her bike to meet Shane for almost a year now, so that was not a big deal anymore. In the beginning, the rendezvous had been so thrilling, so fun, the best time of her life. There had been a few rocky times. Being in love was more complicated than she had ever imagined, especially when it was forbidden love. It seemed that after that sunset afternoon when something within her had convicted her this was not right, everything had changed. Her happiness had drained into a pool of despair.

She pushed the food away and grunted in disgust at herself. For three months, she had done this push-pull dance with Shane, and she knew it was not fair. Pushing Shane away because God's Word said "thou shalt not" and then running back to her and begging her not to leave was so cruel. Finally, Shane had had enough. She would never forget last night though she would try in a myriad of ways. Shane's words were true and haunting.

***

"Thanks for meeting me, Emory; I know you didn't really want to come."

"It's not that I didn't want to come. It's just that I think you deserve better than what I have been giving you."

"Funny, I have often thought you deserved better than me. I have always been so amazed that we ever became friends to start with. I'm a poor kid with very little to offer except a joke or two along the way. And you are good and kind and so much more than I could ever hope to be."

"Shane, stop putting yourself down. You always do that. You are talented and beautiful and funny. You make me smile, Shane. That's what first attracted me to you."

"I haven't been making you smile much lately, have I, Emory? I sure do miss that beautiful smile of yours. I miss so many things we used to do together. I miss just being with you in complete happiness. Emory, I know you are confused and hurting."

"And I am hurting you, too, Shane, and that's the last thing I ever wanted to do."

"Yes, I am hurting, too, but not the way you think. It hurts me to see you so miserable. I've come to the hardest decision I have ever made in my life, but it is the only way. Emory, I'm leaving. I am not even going to finish school. I'll just get my GED later. I'm going back to California. I leave tomorrow morning."

"Shane, no, you can't leave me. You promised me you would never leave me. I'll do better, but I can't lose you. You promised, Shane."

"I promised you also that I would always love you, and loving someone requires sacrifice sometimes. The most loving thing I can do for you is get out of your life. You are eating yourself up inside because of me. I will never ask you to change who you are and what you believe. I know God loves us both. I just am not convinced that our love is wrong. I don't think anything could ever convince me that something so good, so perfect, is wrong. But I'm not you, and I know you, Emory. You have to stay true to what you believe."

"No, Shane. Please just give me a little more time to work through this. I don't want to face a single day in this world without you."

Shane's resolve was shaken, but she maintained her composure. She lifted Emory's chin to look fully at her. "You are the best thing that has ever happened to me, and you will always have a piece of my heart. Goodbye, Emory. I will never forget you."

Emory watched through tear-drenched eyes as Shane walked away—those long ambling strides so familiar to her and the blonde hair flowing down her back that Emory had stroked a thousand times. She never looked back, not even a glance. Emory stood motionless, having no will to go on living.

***

She did not recall exactly how she had made her way to the diner that morning. Everything after Shane left was a blur, but here she sat, alone and utterly devastated. Looking at her hands, she saw Shane's ring that she had worn for more than two years. Numb and confused, she sat lost in thought until a group of cross-country runners came in loudly, jarring her into reality.

She watched the girls all dressed alike, high-five each other, and laugh at silly jokes. Their friendships and fun slapped her in the face, and she hated them for it. Bitterness sought a place to take root in her heart, and the soil there was ripe for it.

She turned away in harrowing grief and saw on the other side of the diner a family with two small girls. The little ones were laughing as their dad was drawing funny faces on the pancakes with the syrup. Their mom watched and helped them cut the cakes so they could eat them.

Mom, Dad, I need you, she said to herself. With supernatural strength, she got up and went to the counter, "May I use your phone, please. It's kind of important."

The elderly lady smiled at her. "Sure, honey, it's right there in my office. And, dear, whatever it is, it will all work out."

Stunned, Emory managed a thank you and walked to the office. She dialed and waited. When her mom answered, she could barely speak, but by God's grace, she found her voice.

***

"Emory?" Shocked and confused, Josie tried to process what was happening. "Emory, it's eight o'clock in the morning. Where are you? Are you all right? Are you in trouble?"

"Mom, listen to me. I am okay, and I'm not in any trouble. But I have something I need to tell you and Dad together in person. I will explain everything to you when I get home but don't worry. I will be home soon."

"Where are you? We can pick you up."

"No, Mom, just let me do it my way, please."

"Okay, honey, we will be here for you. Please be careful. We love you."

Josie returned the receiver, shaken but relieved that Emory was finally going to open up to them. Now they would at least know and be able to help her.

"Josie! Josie!" Lee came running down the stairs at breakneck speed. "Josie, it's Emory. She's not in her room. Where could she be? We've got to go look for her. What is Shane's number? We will try there first."

"Lee, listen to me. Emory just called. She is on the way home and wants to talk to both of us. I think this is the break we have been hoping for. Now don't ask me a lot of questions about where she is or how long she has been gone. I don't know. She only told me she would be home soon and she is okay and not in any kind of trouble."

Relief swept over Lee. "Oh, thank you, Lord, thank you."

"I've been praying for her this morning, Lee, and I think he is answering those prayers.

Twenty minutes later, Emory walked in bundled in her school jacket and gloves. She looked scared and broken. Josie jumped up and ran to her. "Emory, sweetheart, we are so glad you are home."

Before another word was spoken, the phone rang again. Lee reached up to answer it, determined to make it a short call.

"Hello?"

"Dad, it's Eva. Dad, the babies are coming, and I can't reach Rick. He was called in to the shop this morning. Dad, help me! I'm not due for another two weeks, but I, ohhhh, hurry, Dad! I need mom to help me. She knows what I need. Please, Dad, you guys come now!"

"Eva, we are on our way. We will be there in ten minutes. You just hang in there. We are on the way!"

He slammed down the phone and turned to Emory and Josie. "Come on, girls. We have to go help get

154

some babies delivered."

Josie grabbed Emory. "Let's go, Emory. Your sister needs us."

Emory wanted to say no. She wanted to stay there and tell them all about her secrets and all about her horrible sins. But how could she now? The babies were coming whether she liked the timing or not. So, she turned off her emotions again and rode with the family to Eva's house.

Chapter 19
Shamed to Silence

*W*hen Sunday morning broke, it brought with it an early spring rain. The showers pelted Emory's window and woke her from a turbulent sleep. The past twenty-four hours had been a complete blur. In short, she had lost the love of her life in the early-morning hours and become an aunt to two beautiful, healthy babies in the late-night hours.

Even in her grief, she was touched by the new babies. So small, so innocent, she even caught herself saying a prayer for both of them, praying that they would never have to experience the pain she was going through. The thought of their innocence brought her broken heart tonic to combat the bitterness trying to wedge its way in. Even watching her own mom with them did not bring jealousy, but fond memories of times long gone.

The untimely delivery had kept her from confessing her secret, and now she was second-guessing that decision. She did need help. She needed someone to talk to, but what would people think? An associate pastor and a respected homemaker having a lesbian daughter? What a scandal! Especially now in their most proud moment, how could she darken their joy with her sins? Maybe she should wait and try to work it out alone, but she determined that she was going to tell them one day.

"Emory, are you about ready?"

She composed herself, put on a brave face, and opened the door, showing she was fully dressed and ready for church. "All ready, Dad."

"You look beautiful, Emory, and you are on time. You need to teach your mother how to do that."

"Where is Mom?"

"She decided to go back to the hospital instead of to church this morning. Not sure those babies are going to have a chance at not being spoiled."

"You are going to be just as guilty!"

Emory sat by herself in church as she watched her dad on the platform seated with the choir director. Church had become a stranger to her though she had never stopped going. Shane never took her up on that first invitation, and Emory had never invited her again. So Emory kept coming—the hypocrite and liar that she was. She kept smiling and playing happy Christian.

The choir director got up to lead the congregation in the first hymn. Emory could not even mouth the words. She was sick in her soul, and all she wanted to do was run out of this place. She looked again at her dad, a beloved pastor, and then the thoughts and accusations came full throttle: *How could you even think about telling your dad what you have been up to for the past two years. Do you want to destroy the family name and bring shame on your dad? What will people think? You will all have to leave this town. It will cost your dad his job, and he will have to leave the Teen Center that he started—all because of you; if you let anyone know, you will be responsible for ruining the family you claim to love.*

Her dad's voice pierced her thoughts. "Good morning, everyone. On behalf of my family, I just want to announce that as of eleven ten last night, the Johnsons now have a new grandson and a new granddaughter!"

The crowd broke into applause. "A double blessing, Pastor," someone shouted.

"Indeed, it is a double blessing, and we give all praise and glory to our Lord. We want to thank you all, too, for what you have done to prepare for this day. Now, as you know, Pastor Timothy is traveling this morning, so it is my honor to introduce to you our guest speaker, Reverend Eli Samford."

"Reverend Samford is an evangelist who travels the country to spread the good news to all. He has written two books, and he is married with three grown children who are here with us today. Reverend, come and share the message with us."

Emory watched as the huge man climbed the steps to the pulpit. He must have carried at least three hundred pounds on him. She fought the impulse to be repulsed by his obesity. *Who in all the world am I to judge?* Her inner chastisement was dispersed when his booming voice reverberated through the sanctuary.

"You will find that I am a man who gets right to the point, and today I want to talk to you about family. There is a song about being so glad to be part of the family of God. I am sure you all know it well. Well, I hope you are glad, but I hope you are also vigilant in your protection of your family. There is a move afoot in this world today to rip our families apart, and it is a move that is gaining approval in society and the government.

The movement is brought to us under the guise of

love and acceptance, but it is an insidious evil. The homosexuals are trying to trade the truth for lies, as it says in the first chapter of the book of Romans. Their vile and disgusting lust cannot be allowed to penetrate our lives. We must fight the evil they try to spread, for they are agents of the devil himself."

Emory sucked in her breath from the metaphysical punch to her gut, to her soul. She watched the Reverend's face grow red and wet with perspiration. He did not say as much as he spewed his diatribe.

"The book of Leviticus tells us twice that homosexuality is an abomination. That word means it is so foul and disgusting to our Lord that it will draw his judgment. We can now see that judgment in a disease he has inflicted upon the gays. AIDS is the gays' judgment; his judgment for trading in his natural will for the perversion they engage in."

Emory wanted to disappear into the pew. Shame washed over her and crushed her spirit. She looked at her dad on the platform. He sat with a look of disbelief on his face. Whatever he was thinking, she knew he would never understand her choices and sinful behavior.

"Listen to me, brothers and sisters. Yes, be glad we are all a part of the family of God, but be assured, too, that there is no place in this family for the homosexual. This truth is in the Word, not from me. Clearly, the gays will be a part of the masses that find their eternity in the pit of hell. This will be their ultimate and just end."

Fear swept through Emory. She had known that she was a sinner, engulfed in one of the worst of sins, but never had she thought she was going to hell. She prayed a silent prayer of repentance, "Lord,

I am sorry for turning away from you, but I believe you have saved me, and I am going to be with you in eternity. I am sorry for everything, and I promise you I will do everything I can to never do this again. But Lord, please take these feelings away. I don't want to have these attractions, Lord. Take them from me. I love you, Lord, and I know that you love me."

Emory was quiet on the ride home, the brave front for her dad eroded by the words of a zealous preacher. She stole a couple of glances at her dad, who seemed to be in deep thought. He pulled the car into the drive and parked next to Josie's car.

Lee and Emory walked into the house. Josie was at the stove cooking again. He leaned over and gave her a kiss on the cheek. "So, how is everybody doing at the hospital?"

"Great news! They have been discharged and are at home, tired but doing well."

"Already? Wow, that is amazing!"

"Yeah, I think the insurance company doesn't like to pay any more than they have to, so they like to get them out of there as soon as possible. But they are really doing great. They're beautiful. I thought it was time for me to leave and give Rick and Eva some alone time with each other and the babies without a doting grandma hovering over them all. Sorry I missed church."

"Don't be," Lee responded coolly.

"What do you mean by that, Lee?"

"Oh, we had a guest preacher today, and he was horrible. We need to screen our speakers better, but we had heard good reports about him."

"What was wrong with him?"

"Let's just say he is the kind of guy who passes

judgment on people he does not even know. He is one of those all-truth-and-no-love guys. I just hope he didn't harm anyone with his words of damnation today."

"I am glad I wasn't there. The devil holds enough people in the bondage of shame without a misguided man of God helping him."

"Dad," Emory ventured. "What that man said today about gay people going to hell, is that true?"

"Honey, what is true is that anyone who chooses to do his or her will above God's shall not spend eternity with Him. If a gay person rejects Jesus as Savior and Lord, then, yes, they will be denied entry into heaven. First Corinthians, chapter six, says that homosexuals will not inherit the kingdom of God. But it does not single out that sin alone. It also includes the greedy, thieves, slanderers, swindlers, and those who practice all forms of sexual impurity. Too many people like Revered Samford want to only focus on homosexuals, and they leave out the rest of that passage, which says that some of you were such as these, but by God's grace, you are washed and sanctified and justified. The key is the word "were." See, honey, God sees all our sins as an affront to his holiness. It is only the blood of Jesus that can substitute our sin for his righteousness. That's what justified means. If not for Jesus' death on the cross, there is no one ever born who would go to heaven. On our own, we are lost and unworthy, but we are made perfect in Christ."

"But, Dad, once we are saved, why do we keep on sinning?"

"That's a good question, Emory. The answer is that as long as we are in this world, we have a sin nature. There is a battle going on in us all the time. God gives us free will, which means he allows us to choose his will or follow our own desires. In this world, sin is attractive. In the short term, it is exciting and fun and profitable, but it eventually leads to some really bad consequences."

Emory drank in all her dad explained to her. Her earlier prayer was on the right track then. She had to choose God always, no matter how strong her feelings were. Her resolve was cemented; the past must be kept forever a secret. If she could do that, then everything would be okay.

"Thanks, Dad. I think I understand. I am glad you explained that to me."

Lee took Emory by the hand. "Honey, come here a minute." They walked to the dining table and sat down as Lee looked at Josie.

Understanding the inference, Josie turned the stove off and moved the skillet off the hot eye. She wiped her hands and joined them.

Lee continued, "Emory, while we are talking, is there something you want to tell us? We want you to know you can tell us anything because we love you, sweetheart. Before all of the excitement with the babies, you said you wanted to talk to us. You have our undivided attention."

Emory looked at Lee and then Josie. She could not recall the last time that just the three of them had really been together. Sure, they had dinner every night, but after Eva left, it seemed like Emory had left the table, too.

She swallowed hard and tried to think of an improvised reason for telling them she needed to talk. So much had happened in such a short period of time, and especially after that sermon, she was never going to tell them or anyone else about her secret. No, she would bury that and take it to her grave. Only she and God would know.

"Well, I guess you have noticed that I've been having a not-so-happy time around here the last few months. I've just been needing a change, you know, some new friends, new challenges."

Josie reached over and touched her arm, "Go on, honey, we are listening."

"What I wanted to ask you about was, well, I want to graduate from high school early. I only need two more classes, and I can take them this summer. Then I could enroll in college in the fall."

Lee and Josie looked at each other, both taken completely off guard. Lee shifted in his seat and tried to not show his disapproval of the idea without hearing Emory out.

"But what about your senior year? That is the very best year in high school, and you still have another basketball season. Coach says you could really improve your chances of getting a scholarship to a big-name school with a good senior year."

"Dad, my senior year will just be a waste of time. I'd be bored silly. But I do want to play ball in college. I've even gotten an offer from State College, and I've decided that is where I want to go. It's only a couple of hours away. I can still easily come home on some weekends and holidays. I've already met the coach and like her. She says I would get a lot of playing time even in my first year. What do you think?"

Josie's turn, "Emory, it's evident you have already given this a lot of thought, but it is such a surprise to us. We need time to absorb it and talk it over some more before we can give you an answer. This all seems so sudden, though. Did something happen to trigger it?"

"No, no, not just one thing. It's just a lot of things over a long period of time. I am just so restless, especially at school."

"I am not sure how to ask this," Lee chimed, "but I feel like I need to just to be able to help you."

"Go ahead, Dad."

"Does this have anything to do with how the team came up short this year in the title run. I mean, are the kids giving you a hard time or bullying you about getting beat in the Regionals?"

"Oh no, no, Dad. Nothing like that. No one has said anything to me about that at all. We were all just really disappointed. I'm trying to tell you both this is something in me, something that makes me feel like I don't fit in here anymore. I really don't know how to describe it."

"What about this family? Do you feel you fit with us?' Josie asked.

Emory thought before she answered. If she told them the truth, she would needlessly hurt them, and she would have to explain everything. That wasn't going to happen. She really did not fit with anyone except Shane, but that had to change, and she was determined that it would.

"Of course, Mom, you are my family. And now we will have two more in the family for all those famous holiday dinners of yours," she deflected. "Please let me do this. I really think it would help me."

Relieved but still not completely convinced they had been told everything, Josie stood up and moved to Emory's side of the table. "Come here, daughter."

Josie engulfed her in her arms and pulled her snuggly to her. "You know we love you."

Lee stood and joined the hug. "Yes, we do, more than you know."

Emory returned her parents' hugs, grudgingly and with bittersweet memories tempering the attention they now showered upon her. A strange mixture of feelings collided in her heart and mind. *Why couldn't you have done this when I needed you instead of taking care of everyone but me? Where were you when Pepper died when my world was devastated? No, you were not here, but Shane was. You say you love me, but Eva is the one you truly love. Your words are hollow. Shane's words were true and wonderful.*

She managed a muffled and insincere, "I love you, too," just to escape from the unwanted group hug. Emory pulled back first and looked to her dad.

"So, is it all right for me to graduate earlier and move on to college?"

"Now, Emory, like your mom said, we need a little time to process this, but if it is what you really want, we will see. If we feel that it is okay, you know we will always support you."

"Thanks, Dad, Mom. I know once you have time to consider it, you will see what I mean. I'll need to do a lot of things to make it happen, so don't take too long."

"Okay, Emory, we promise we will let you know soon. But look, I don't want you to do anything on your own just yet. We want to know more about the college and the coach and all of those things. We want to feel comfortable with living arrangements and all the new things that will be part of your life,"

"Sure, I will need you to help with all kinds of stuff,

but please say yes. I'm going up to see Pepper on the hill now while you think it over."

Josie was the first to speak after the door slammed behind Emory. "Seeing her so excited after more than a year of depression is enough to convince me that maybe it would be best to let her go. What do you think?"

"Yeah, it sure was nice to see her looking forward to something. You know, for so long, it seems like she had just lost interest in life as if something had sucked all her hope and joy out of her."

"You're right. It's been hard to see her like that, but I blame us a little. We have been so preoccupied with Eva, her marriage, the babies, everything."

"Now, Josie, we can't be blamed for loving both our kids, and Eva really needed us. I mean, if she and Rick had not worked things out, there would be no babies."

"Oh, I can't imagine no Daniel and Hannah. Still, I just wish I had done more for Emory. But I know you are right. We cannot live their lives for them. That's so hard, Lee."

"I know, honey, but I think we have decided, haven't we?"

"Yes, we have to let her go. But like you told her, Lee, we are going to be involved with the whole move, and we can try to go to some of her games, right?'

"Of course, a few road trips for the old grandparents will keep us young—that and chasing some toddlers around all the time."

"Now who is rushing everything?"

Lee laughed, "Come on. Let's dish out some of that lunch you have made and make another one of our children happy today."

Chapter 20
Kelly to the Rescue

1983, 18 years old

$\mathscr{S}$weaty and tired, Emory lugged her books and gym bag up the stairs to her second-floor dorm room. She had been assigned to Room 252 three weeks previously when she first arrived at her new school. The roommate assignment was random, and she had drawn a real winner—at least in her mind. Sara had a boyfriend she was basically living with. Emory had seen her all of three times when she swung by to pick up things she needed. Emory, though, was happy with the arrangement. With the room to herself, she could do what she liked, any time she liked.

She juggled all her cargo to find her key. Sliding it in the door, she saw the key chain and thought about how her parents had surprised her with a car just after she finished her summer classes. She could not have picked out a better one, a fire engine red Chevy Citation. After hearing all the warnings and precautions, her dad finally handed her the keys, and the three of them rode around town on the maiden trip.

Emory flipped on the light and flung her bag on the bed. Setting the books on the table, she flopped down next to her bag. She was tired but still had a lot to do: term papers, reading assignments, and memorizing basketball plays. Instead of doing any of them, she reached for her journal and began to read the chronicles of her summer.

Page after page was filled with memories of Shane, with tear-stained ink smearing every emotion on the parchment. Then the words that had become her mantra ended each entry, "The Lord is my God, and I will serve Him. Please, Lord, just take these feelings from me."

She jumped at the knock on her door, a first for her. "Hey, Emory, open up. It's Beth and Tammy."

"Yeah, just a minute. I'm coming." She opened the door to two teammates who had befriended her on the first day of practice. Beth was short but a super quick point guard who could dribble through any double team. Tammy was a shooting forward, the same position Emory would be vying for. They were both juniors but new to the school because of their transfers from a Junior College.

"Hey, guys, what's up?"

"We thought we would go see about the big party at the frat house tonight and decided you needed to come with us."

"Oh no, guys, I've got a lot of stuff I need to do, and I haven't even showered since practice."

"Oh, come on, Emory. It's Friday night. Lighten up, will you? You have got to get out and meet people. That's what college is about."

Not really wanting to go out, especially to a frat house, she relented because she knew they would never give up. "Well, all right, but I'm not staying late."

"Atta' girl. Get your shower. We will wait. And just throw on some jeans and a shirt. It's super casual."

Thirty minutes later, the three walked into Emory's first visit inside a frat house. It was actually a lot nicer than she had expected, but the crowd was pretty wild. She looked around the room and watched as the guys hit on the girls and the girls toyed with them. For her, it was a distasteful game she did not want any part in. Never had she felt more out of place and awkward.

"Hey there, red, how are you tonight? My name is Jim. Can I get you anything to drink?"

Emory turned and saw a tall, geeky-looking guy leaning over her. Apparently, she had been abandoned by her teammates the minute they walked in the door.

"Uh, no, no thanks. I'm fine."

"So, what's your name?"

"I'm Emory, Emory Johnson,"

"Well, Emory Johnson, what's your story?"

"Story?"

"Yeah, you know, where you from? What's your sign? Tell me all your hopes and dreams," Jim laughed at his own clever line.

Emory was so repulsed she wanted to smack him in the face and run. Instead, she backed up, but he stepped with her. Feeling suffocated by his infringement in her space, she spat out the only words that came to her: "Get away from me. Leave me alone."

Apparently, her voice was near a yell as several of the party-goers turned and stared at them. Panic set in, and Emory was unsure of what to do next. She had never experienced anything like this and was not equipped to handle it.

Suddenly, she felt a hand around her shoulder and a voice of rescue, "Jim, why don't you get yourself another drink. Leave this poor girl alone."

"But I didn't do anything. I didn't lay a hand on her."

"Jim, please do it for me. There are a lot of other girls here that I know would love to meet you. Go on now."

"All right. Sure, Kelly, sure."

Emory exhaled. She was embarrassed, but it could have been a lot worse, and she knew it. Finally, she looked at her knight in shining armor and was shocked to see the knight was a girl—not just a girl, but a very attractive one.

"Thanks. You don't know how much I needed help."

"You are welcome. Guys can be such animals. I've been where you were. It's no fun to be on their turf and under their rules. My name is Kelly Hogan."

"Emory Johnson. So why are you here, Kelly? I mean, if you know how these parties are and everything?"

"Ha, that's a very astute question, Emory. I can tell you this much. I'm not here for a pick-up. I've been around this college for a while now, and I come to these events because I have to. It's part of my job."

"Your job is to rescue girls who get themselves in uncomfortable situations?"

"Well, I've never heard it put that way, but yeah, that's a pretty good description of this part of my job. I'm a graduate assistant trainer with the athletic program. This particular frat is one geared toward the athletes, so I am supposed to keep them out of trouble. It's really two-fold. A lot of the girls who come here are also athletes, so I watch both for the girls and the guys. My turn, what brings you here, Emory?"

"Truthfully, I never wanted to come, but a couple of my teammates talked me into coming. I kind of just did it for them so they would quit hounding me. Then, of course, when we got here, they left me alone. You saw the rest."

"What's your sport? Wait, let me guess, basketball. Am I right?"

"Yep, how did you guess?"

"I'm very perceptive, plus I saw you practice today. I always like to swing by and see the new teams. Looks like you guys will be pretty good this year, from what I can tell. The potential is there anyway, and Coach Day is a good coach. She knows her players and uses them well. But let me warn you, she can be pretty tough and can be a really bad loser."

"You know Coach Day?"

"Oh yes, I know Coach Day very well. I think you will like her. Just don't get on her bad side. The worst thing you can possibly do is not give all your effort—that and never, ever question her. She is a bit of a control freak. Just let her be. Never challenge her."

"Wow, thanks, those are some great tips. I'm just a freshman, but I would really like to get some good quality playing time this year. Competition is pretty tight, though."

"Just play hard, be coachable, and be a team player. Believe me, that will get you a long way. While I'm giving advice, can I ask you about something?"

"Sure."

"That right shoulder of yours, have you ever injured it?"

"Why, yes, I have. Say, you really are perceptive."

"Years of experience in treating athletes will do that for you. What happened?"

"I was hit by a car a couple of years ago. Killed my best friend, Pepper, and dislocated my shoulder."

"Aww, Emory, I'm so sorry to hear about your friend."

"Thanks, but I guess I should clarify. See Pepper was my fifteen-year-old dog. I really did love that guy."

"That does not at all diminish my sorrow for you. I had a dog, too, that was my best friend. I could tell Mic anything, and he just accepted me and all my problems. I thought my heart would never heal when he died. It's tough. I am so sorry."

Emory looked at Kelly and knew she genuinely meant every word. She could feel the undercurrent of compassion that let her know Kelly was a good person. "Thank you, that means a lot. Okay, enough of sad memories. Did you notice something about my arm?"

"Yes, I did. When you injured it, did you do any therapy to help heal the stretched ligaments?"

"Not much. No one ever suggested more than a few exercises for it. They just kind of popped it back into place, and as soon as I could bear the pain, I started playing again."

"Uh-huh, I can tell. See, your ligaments are really tight, and when you shoot the ball, your follow-through is shortened because you have never really regained your full range of motion. I believe with some massage therapy and a lot of intense stretching exercises, you can get that full extension back and with it a truer shot."

"Really? Wow! That would be great. I have never really shot as well after that accident, but I just thought it was other things I had on my mind. It was an unsettling time in my life. I couldn't really focus."

"Well, I'll be happy to work with you. I really believe you will see a big difference, and for no extra cost, if you ever have focus issues, I'm here if you need to talk."

"You're very kind, Kelly. You know, I hate the way we met, but I'm glad we did." Emory's words belied the feelings she fought to bury.

"I'm glad we met, too, Emory; I'm looking forward to working with you. Hey, do you feel like leaving this place?"

"Only since I first walked in."

"Good. Let's go. I'll walk you home the long way."

"But what about your job, you know, monitoring the Neanderthals?"

Kelly laughed, "You're funny, Emory, but on the money. They are fine; I'll swing by later and make sure they haven't hazed anybody. It's still early in the evening. They don't get bad until after midnight."

The long way home turned out to be a two-mile trek across campus to places Emory had not known were there. Kelly told her the history of all the buildings and the folklore that came with the storied institution. They passed the football field as Kelly talked about the players she had treated and the things they do to keep them playing even when their bodies were broken. Next was the gymnasium. It was small but well-built.

"One day, we are going to look up at that scoreboard inside and see your name, Emory, and I predict you will be the first all-American in the history of the school."

"Now who is the funny one, hotshot?" Emory laughed easily.

They walked on to Mayweather Hall, Emory's dorm. "Well, here you are. Now, aren't you glad you did get out tonight?"

"It certainly didn't start well, but, yes, Kelly, I'm very glad."

"Good, you take care now. I better get on back to the job. See you on Monday?"

"Yes, absolutely. See you Monday. And, Kelly, thanks again."

"No problem, I enjoyed tonight. I think we are going to be friends."

"Me, too. Good night Sha... I mean Kelly. Be careful."

Emory's eyes lingered on Kelly as she walked away. She wondered what Kelly would look like with her deep brown hair down out of her long ponytail. Smiling, she realized that this was the first time she had genuinely laughed since Shane left. How bizarre it was that she had almost called her Shane. *But it was a good night after all. Now I have a friend finally. That is all we will be, but good friends are a gift, and I hope that is what we are, Kelly.* She spoke only to the night air that filled her lungs like a long-awaited gift.

Unexpectedly, Kelly turned and started walking back toward her. Emory shifted her eyes, fearing her stare had been detected. She stood frozen, hoping she had not been busted as Kelly approached her.

"Emory, good. I'm glad I caught you."

"Yes, what is it?

"Look, this is a little bit awkward for me, but once you get to know me, you will know that I am a pretty blunt person. I just believe in the truth and laying my cards on the table. So, in the interest of full disclosure, I need to tell you something about me. I

176

know this is a little early in our getting to know each other, but I would rather you hear it from me than from someone else."

"Okay, you have definitely piqued my curiosity. What is it?"

"Well, I want you to know, first of all, that if what I tell you is offensive to you, I apologize right up front. If you do not want to be associated with me, I understand that, too, because people can be pretty mean about this sort of thing."

"Kelly, whatever it is, I am sure your friendship with me will not be in jeopardy. I owe you for the rescue tonight, and I just can't imagine anything that would offend me about you."

"Okay, well, with all warnings being given, here goes. Emory, I am gay. I don't flaunt it or try to push it on anyone else, but I accept it, and I embrace it. Not a lot of people know, but I think some of the seniors on the team probably have guessed. The worst part is people who don't know me start making up rumors, and some really nasty and untrue things start flying around. I want to ask you to come to me if you hear things like that. I promise you I will tell you the truth."

Emory swallowed hard, her head spinning and her heart beating fast. She had tried so hard to leave that part of her life behind, and now here it was right back in her face. It wasn't just what Kelly had said. It was much more than that. It was how Kelly made her feel.

"Emory, can you say something? I kind of did a big reveal, and I have no idea what you are thinking. Should I just go now and pretend we never met?"

"No, uh no, no. I am so sorry. I'm just a little surprised."

"Surprised or embarrassed to be seen with me?"

"Not at all. I am just a little blown away by the courage you have to openly admit this to someone you barely know."

"Truthfully, I'm a little surprised myself. There is just something about you that makes me feel like you would understand. But the biggest reason is that I don't want you to be blindsided. I don't want you to get caught up in a bunch of rumors. I felt like you deserve to know, and I don't want you to get hurt."

"That means a lot to me, Kelly, and, yes, I definitely want to be friends. Other people can talk all they want. Who cares? But I do want to ask you a question: what do you think of me?"

"I think I like you. I think you are pretty cool, especially for a freshman, and I think you are going to do very well here at State."

"No, I mean, oh, never mind. Thanks for the vote of confidence."

"You mean, what do my perceptions tell me about whether or not you have same-sex feelings?" Kelly ventured.

"I do," Emory whispered, hardly believing the confession that had just slipped out of her mouth.

"But you are conflicted by what you feel and what you believe to be morally wrong?"

"How do you do that? It's like you are inside my head."

"I am inside your head because when I first came to State, that is where my head was, too. I went through high school a complete misfit with feelings I did not want and could not control. I was awful to my girlfriend because I was so at war within myself. When we broke up, I swore never again to act

178

on any of my feelings. I come from a good Christian family, and I believe in Jesus, so I decided to never allow these feelings to overcome me again. Of course, I failed, but in the process, I learned some really important lessons—like not believing all the interpretations of the Bible that you hear. I know where you are. Just like that shoulder of yours that was never properly treated, your heart has never received the proper treatment it needs. You have healed somewhat, but your healing will never be complete until you face it and talk to someone about it. I can tell you from experience the feelings will not stay buried, no matter how hard you try."

Emory could hardly believe what she was hearing. She felt like a pressure valve had just released years of pent-up tension in her soul. Here was a believer, just like she was, who knew her better than her own parents—heck, better than she knew herself.

Finally, she found her voice, "How did you come to accept that you could be both gay and Christian?"

"Now that, my friend, is a long, long story. But instead of telling you about it, how about if I show you a little bit about how it happened?"

"Show me? What do you mean?"

"How would you like to go to church with me tomorrow afternoon?"

"But tomorrow is Saturday."

"Yes, we have church on Saturday afternoon and again on Sunday morning. It's the same service but just gives people options. Also, our building is small, so we need the room available with two services."

"I'd love to go to church with you. I've been meaning to find a church in this area anyway but just haven't had much time. This is actually the first weekend I have stayed on campus. I usually go home. You know, Mom and Dad worry."

"Oh, yes, I know. My folks still call me once or twice a week. So we are set. I'll swing by your dorm around one-thirty tomorrow to take you to All Comers Fellowship on Maple."

"That's a unique name for a church!"

"Yep, we just added the 'on Maple' to fancy it up. It is a unique name for a unique congregation. You will see what I mean. I think you will really enjoy it. Do you want me to come up to your room or meet you out here?"

"Why don't you come on up if you don't mind. I don't really have a roommate, and you can check out the cool freshman's pad."

"Great, I will see you tomorrow. We are very casual. Some come dressed in suits and dresses, but most of us just wear whatever we were going to put on that day."

"I'm in Room 252, second door on the right when you reach the top of the stairs."

"Got it. See you then."

Again, Kelly strode off with that long confident gait. Again, Emory watched her, not caring this time if she were to be busted for staring. After several minutes, she climbed the stairs and heard the phone in her room ringing. Quickly unlocking the door, she reached it just in time.

"Hello?"

"Hey, Emory, it's Mom."

"Hey, Mom, why are you calling this late?"

"The kids are being dedicated at the church tomorrow, and we want so much for you to come."

"Oh no, I'm sorry. I'd love to be there, but I just

can't make it tomorrow. Take lots of pictures and tell everyone I am sorry. I hate to miss the big day. Yes, everything is going really great. Okay, love you, too."

She hung up the phone and looked in the mirror. It was the first time in a long while that she really felt like everything was truly going well.

Chapter 21
Opposite Directions

"Come on, Josie. We are going to be late," Lee called from the running car.

"Okay, okay, I'm coming. I had to get the camera."

Josie got in the car, and Lee smiled at her. Putting the car in reverse, they backed out of the driveway and headed for the church.

"You look beautiful, Josie, but far too young to be a grandma."

"Lee, you say the sweetest things to me sometimes. Daniel and Hannah are so lucky to have a grandpa like you. I am just so disappointed that Emory couldn't make it."

"I'm sure she would be here if she could, dear. We really did not give her much notice."

"Oh, I know, but we didn't know until last night. Who could have predicted that Pastor Tim was going to be called out of town? I am glad he could do it today. But I am sorry Emory can't be there. She really likes being around those babies."

"I know, honey, but she has other obligations now. So how did she sound when you talked with her? Is she starting to get more comfortable?"

"Lee, she sounded wonderful—the happiest I have heard her in a very long time. It was almost as if she had gotten her joy back."

"You got all of that in a ten-minute conversation?"

"It was just her tone, her energy. It was like she had things to look forward to after so many months of depression. Just call it mother's intuition."

Lee laughed, "I'll call it good news and leave it at that."

They pulled into the church parking lot after the short, familiar drive and saw several cars already there. Walking in, they were met at the door by Pastor Tim.

"The grandparents are here. All is well," he laughed.

Lee extended a hand, "Wouldn't miss it for the world, brother. Looks like a really amazing turnout for a Saturday morning, late-notice ceremony."

"Yes, you can thank my secretary and the deacons for getting the word out quickly. As for the response, you can thank all the good people who think so highly of your family. More than that, they realize the importance of raising our children to love the Lord."

"Amen, Pastor. Thank you for doing this."

"It's my honor, Lee. Emory is not with you?

"No, unfortunately, she couldn't make it."

"You have two wonderful girls, Lee. Wish we had baby dedications back when your kids were born. They are so important, but I know you raised them right."

"Tim, I am a rich man indeed. I hope to see these two little ones baptized one day like my girls were when they were kids."

"The church needs to wake up and really start discipling young ones after they receive Christ as Savior. I'm afraid we have a tendency to lead them to salvation and then do very little to help them dedicate all of the rest of their life to Christ. That's one reason we started these dedications."

"You're right. The world has a lot of crazy and deceitful theologies out there. I pray every day that Emory does not fall prey to any of them."

"Are you worried she might?"

"No specific reason to think she would, but she is away from home. She is still very young. Josie keeps having uneasy thoughts about Emory being on her own."

"Well, you let me know if there is anything I can do to help. I've known Emory since the day she was born, and she is a very special part of this church family. I will pray for her, too."

"Thank you, Pastor Tim. I'll let you go now. Guess I better go find the guests of honor."

Lee walked into the half-full sanctuary. Fresh flowers adorned the entire front of the church, and candles lit the dais. He spotted Josie right away, already talking to Eva and Rick, each holding a baby. He quickly pulled out the camera and captured a candid shot. To him, they were the best kind.

"Hey there, everyone, are we all set?"

"Daddy!" Eva leaned over and gave him a kiss on his cheek. "Thank you for pulling all of this together. It is all so beautiful."

"Eva, I'd love to take the credit, but I did not have a hand in any of this. This is all thanks to the deacons and the ladies of the church. Now let me see those precious little ones."

Hannah was dressed in a white gown that covered even her feet. It was punctuated with lace and embroidery. Lee immediately saw his wife's design in it. Daniel had on a light blue suit complete with a tiny cross lapel pin sown into the fabric. This he knew was Eva's handiwork.

"They are so adorable," Josie gushed. "Lee, you've got the camera, right? Take several of them up close."

Lee managed to get a couple of shots before the ceremony began. The family stood with Pastor Tim as he said a few words of introduction and then offered a prayer:

"Lord, we come before you to dedicate these children, Daniel Lee Smith and Hannah Josephine Smith, to you. We do this in obedience to your command that we raise our children to know and to love the Lord with all their hearts, minds, souls, and strength. We thank you, Father, for the gifts that these young ones are, and we pray for your presence, peace, and protection all the days of their lives. In Jesus name, we pray, and all God's people said:"

"Amen," echoed through the sanctuary.

"Thank you all for coming to be a part of this service. We have these dedication ceremonies because we believe that it is of vital importance that the church pledge to be a part of the teaching and nurturing of our children."

Pastor Tim walked over and stood between Rick and Eva. "I've known these two for many years now, and I know the kind of parents they will be. Normally, I would hold the child to be dedicated, but my dexterity is questionable, especially for trying to hold two at once."

Laughter rippled through the crowd as the two children started to squirm right on cue. Seeing the restlessness that was already setting in, the Pastor pressed on.

"Rick and Eva, do you promise to love these children with all your heart and to take care and protect them at all times?

186

"We do."

"And do you promise before God and all of these witnesses to teach your children about the love of Jesus that led Him to die for our sins?"

"We do."

"And will you always live a life as an example to them of godly men and women and uphold the biblical commands and instructions of the Holy Word?"

"We will."

"Very good. Now, church, you need to make your pledge of support to the

Smith family. Will you promise to pray for this family, for their physical and spiritual wellbeing?"

"We will."

"Will you help them teach their children about the love of Jesus?"

"We will."

"And will you provide sound biblical counsel to these young parents in all of their efforts to raise Daniel and Hannah?"

"We will."

"Very good. Now Rick and Eva, these promises that have been made today are a sacred covenant made before God. Your children are going to be confronted with things of this world that can lead them astray, but you must always let your children know that they can trust you. Communication is vital, and your love needs to be shown to them every day. Being a parent is the most challenging of all professions, but it is also the most rewarding. You will not be able to do this by yourself. Always remember that your family and your church are here for you. Above all else, always depend upon the Holy Spirit to guide you in wisdom and discernment. As your children grow older, each phase of growth will bring new and different opportunities for you to make mistakes, which indeed you will. But mistakes are not insurmountable. It is very important, too, that you show no partiality. Treat them as the unique individuals that they are. God will give you the strength, the stamina, the patience, and the courage you need as long as you lean on Him."

"Rick and Eva, do you fully understand and accept this challenge that has been given to you, and do you dedicate your children, Daniel and Hannah, wholly and completely to the Lord?"

"We do."

"And now everyone, we have a little something extra today to close our ceremony. If you would like to step across the way to the fellowship hall, our ladies have prepared some freshly baked goodies and coffee for all—and I do mean fresh just out of the oven!"

Josie dabbed her eyes and thanked everyone who came up to congratulate her. She kept telling Lee to take more pictures. Together the family walked to the refreshment table. Through it all, Josie could not stop thinking about her other daughter, who had missed all of this.

That night as they went to bed, she curled up into Lee's arms and sighed, "Lee, I have been thinking a lot about Emory today. I feel like the Holy Spirit is telling me we really need to pray hard for her. There is just this feeling I get that she is in the middle of a spiritual battle. I'm afraid she is not equipped for it."

Chapter 22
Delusion of Freedom

*E*mory was excited. She woke early and went for a run in the cool autumn air. Tracing the route of her nocturnal walk with Kelly, she ran faster until her lungs burned. She needed to build up stamina in this higher altitude, and buoyed by thoughts of her new friend, she pressed harder. Her shoulder ached when she pumped her arms. She thought of the possibilities of a fully healed shoulder. Sprinting to the front of the dorm, she put her hands on her hips and bent over, completely spent. Never in her life had she pushed herself so hard, but it felt good. She felt good. She felt alive again.

Good job, Emory, she encouraged herself. *You have earned a shower and a really good breakfast."*

Self-rewarded with good food and a soaking scrub, she sat at the window, allowing the sun to warm her face. This was going to be a good day. She tried off and on to study, but her eye continued to wander to the clock. Time went by slowly as she processed her conversation with Kelly and her sheer joy in having met someone who not only understood her but embraced her. But still, there was much healing and doubt that lingered.

The knock at the door startled her. Taking only a moment to catch her breath, she opened it to see a smiling Kelly. Her hair was down, and it was, as imagined, really beautiful. Seeing her in the light of day was a whole new experience. Her eyes were a deep chocolate brown, and her skin was well tanned, but it was that smile that was captivating.

"Hey, Emory."

"Hey, Kelly, come on in. I am ready, but I wanted to show you a couple of pictures if we have time."

"Sure, I love pictures."

Emory pulled down two photographs, and Kelly's smile grew bigger. "Don't tell me. Bet I know who this is. It's got to be your beloved Pepper. Oh, he looks so happy with you."

"That describes him perfectly. He was one happy dog."

"Guess that's because he knew how lucky he was to have you."

"Yeah, he was well treated. And this one is taken up on the hill we used to walk. I think he had just spotted a squirrel. See how his ears are all perked up."

"Nothing better than a good dog. They just give you love. No judgments, no criticisms, no arguments. They never have to have their way."

"Honestly, Kelly, if it had not been for Pepper, I probably would not be here today."

"Did you ever wish you were not alive, Emory? Ever think it would just be a lot easier to die? At least then, the pain would go away, right?"

"I've never had anyone ask me that before, but yes."

"Because of how you felt about another girl?"

"Yes, it broke my heart when Shane left. But it wasn't her fault. It was all mine. I just could not get past the conflicting feelings of love and guilt."

"Good."

"Good, you call that good? Did you hear what I just said?

"Yes, and it's good that you were able to say it and get it out in the open. I'm sure you have felt like a tormented prisoner with that all bottled up inside for so long. That is what is good about it, and even better, we can help you."

"We? Who? How?"

"Listen, just come with me to church. You will find out what I mean. I know. I was so much like you, but now I am one of the happiest people you will ever meet—almost as happy as Pepper here."

They drove in a new Ford truck Kelly had saved for three years to buy. Listening to music and talking about sports and cars along the short drive from campus, the girls soon arrived at their destination. Kelly turned right onto Maple Street and pulled into the parking lot of a small brick church. It was immaculately kept and had a large sign in front that read "All Comer's Fellowship Church" followed in smaller letters with the words, "We welcome and love everyone."

Emory got out of the truck, feeling both nervous and excited. She did not know what to expect, but she was hoping to find peace and joy about who she was, just as Kelly had. Two greeters met them at the front and smiled broadly at her. "Welcome, thank you for being our guest today. We are so glad you could join us."

She looked at the mostly full pews and was floored by what she saw. Men sat with their male partners and women with girlfriends. There were people of all ages and ethnicities exchanging pleasantries and blessings with one another. Were it not for the pairing of same-gender couples, this would look like a miniature version of her church at home.

A couple walked up to where they were standing, and Kelly hugged each of them. "Mary, Stacy, I'd like you to meet a new friend of mine. This is Emory. She is a freshman this year, and once I get her shoulder properly healed, she is going to be a standout for the basketball team."

Stacy reached over and gave Emory a big hug, followed by Mary, who said, "So glad to meet you. We hope you enjoy the service. Stacy and I have some things to take care of today, but maybe in the future, we can go out to eat after church. Oh, and Emory, I have to tell you, you are in good hands with this one. She can work magic on healing anything that ails you."

"Now, Mary, don't raise the bar so high I can never meet it."

Emory laughed, surprised at how relaxed she immediately felt. "It's nice to meet you both. Yeah, I am trusting Kelly to make me the star she thinks I can be."

The piano struck a chord indicating it was time to begin the service. All four girls found a pew and crowded into it. Emory kept looking around to take it all in. The pulpit was emblazoned with a carving of the cross. Behind it was a small choir loft that featured about a dozen robed singers.

Introductions and announcements were followed by four praise and worship songs, all of which Emory knew by heart. Feeling more at home with each passing moment, she was looking forward to hearing the speaker.

"Good morning, everyone. For those of you who are visiting with us today, my name is Reverend Mark Turner, and I am so happy that we have gathered together to bring glory to our Savior, Jesus Christ. We are a body of believers who love the Lord and each other. There is enough hate and vitriol in this world, especially for us, so it is always wonderful to spend time together in this sanctuary."

"We live today no longer under the law but under the new covenant, under the grace of God. And though we, who happen to love someone of our own gender, are often hated and vilified, we are called to love even our enemies. So we obey, and we pray for eyes to be opened to the love of Jesus for all."

Mark walked from behind the lectern and looked directly at those in the pews in front of him. He smiled and continued, "Jesus said, 'Let him who has no sin cast the first stone.' After that, the only sound was the thud of dropped stones and sandals retreating on the dusty path. There was no one left to stone the condemned woman."

"Today, there are many who say that no homosexual will ever enter the kingdom of God. We know that is a lie from the devil, for it is God Himself who blessed us with this gift and made us just the way we are. They base their views on such Scriptures as Leviticus 18, which calls homosexuality an abomination. Closer study shows that idolatry is what is being referred to in these passages. This is seen in the story of Sodom and Gomorrah, where it is not homosexuality that is judged by God. What is being judged and punished is extreme disregard for the wellbeing of others and an effort to rape the visitors to these cities. Yet, those who hate us use these Scriptures as a blanket condemnation calling for God's wrath to come down on us. But we know better. We know God blesses all loving and committed relationships under the new covenant of his grace."

"The arguments made by those who hate us are without merit and distort the Word of God. There can be no doubt that this is true, for if this were such a vile and horrible sin, would not Jesus have addressed it? Surely, he would, but he doesn't mention one word about it."

"No, my friends, those who hate and fear us have fallen for misinterpretations of the Scripture. They are wrong, but we do not hate them; rather, we seek to have open discussions with them to get to know each other on a more intimate basis. I believe that one day they shall begin to understand that we are people just like they are who love the Lord and love our chosen mates. Then on that day, they will drop their stones."

He paused and continued, "Now there may be some here today who are conflicted about their feelings. The conflicts have been brought about by condemning churches and society and family members who call us perverts and deviants and tell us we are going to hell. Listen to me carefully, dear ones. They are wrong. Look around you and see the love that radiates on the faces of everyone here. Recall the praise and worship we have experienced here today. God has made everyone exactly as he intends for each of us to be. All we have to do is accept his blessing and live life to the fullest."

"Okay, let's end with one more song and as you leave here today, go in peace, go in joy, go in love. Grace and peace to you all."

The final hymn over, Emory sat mesmerized by everything that she had heard. Her heart, her mind, her everything felt so liberated. Years of suffering and needless grief evaporated. She looked at Kelly and her friends and knew now why they were so happy, for now, she was, too.

"Well, what did you think?" Kelly beamed at her.

"I, I'm speechless. I thought it was the most wonderful sermon I have ever heard. It feels like this is the first time I truly understand how good God is. I can't believe how free I feel."

"It is beyond words, I know. Are you happy you came?"

"What do you think? I'm ecstatic. I want to come back again to meet more people and to become a part of this church."

"That's great. We would love to have you, but, Emory, I have to warn you. You may accept yourself like never before, but there is a cruel and hate-filled world out there that still sees you as depraved. I just want to warn you to guard yourself. Don't go out and just tell everyone you are gay. This is a very close community of people. If one of us hurts, we all do. So just be careful, and if you will allow me, I will help you navigate through all of this."

"Yes, please, I need all the help I can get. I would never want to hurt you or anyone else."

"Yeah, a lot of people here could lose their job if they were ever outed. To be honest, I took quite a risk bringing you here when I don't know you very well. But you reminded me so much of what I have experienced that I thought it was worth the risk. Come on. Let's walk to the car. I think they want us to clear out."

The short walk gave Emory time to think. All of it seemed like a dream that someone like her would never dare to wish for. She also had time to work up her courage. Closing the truck door, she looked directly into Kelly's big brown eyes and asked the question she had wanted to ask last night.

"Kelly," she paused.

"Yeah, Emory?"

"Do you have a girlfriend?

Kelly's eyes crinkled as her smile broadened. "That's a whole story in itself, Emory. I'll give you details later, but to answer your question, no, I don't have a girlfriend at the moment. I did have a girl-friend, but we broke up about two months ago after a year-long relationship. She just decided one day that she didn't want to be with me anymore. I think she was seeing someone else or at least wanted to break up so she could. It certainly did not take her long to get into another relationship."

"Did she hurt you?"

"It always hurts when you think you know some-one and you give them a piece of yourself, just to be rejected later. Yes, she hurt me, but she did not devastate me. I have no hard feelings toward her. I wish her well."

"How do you do that?"

"Do what?"

"Recover from something like that?"

"It's not as easy as I am making it sound, but it is not impossible either. I think the key is that you have to love yourself and have confidence in who you are. Until you are solid with yourself, it is very dan-gerous to try to have a relationship with someone else. That is when people can get badly hurt and become suicidal."

"I have a lot to learn from you, Kelly. I want to learn to love without fear."

"I can't teach you everything. Life has to do that. I will, though, teach you from my mistakes so you can bypass them."

"Kelly, thank you. Thank you for everything."

"You are welcome; I wish someone could have helped me when I was eighteen and confused."

"You say that like you are an old lady. How old are you anyway?"

"I'm twenty-two and mature beyond my years. I'm also the best trainer in the country, and you are one lucky girl to have me,"

"Yes, Kelly, I am one lucky girl to have you. I really am."

Chapter 23
Parties & Parting

1990, 25-years-old

*E*mory packed her books though she knew she would have no real time to do work over the weekend. This case was more important than any the law firm had allowed her to work, and it stood to impact the lives of so many, including her.

One day she hoped to go to law school and become an attorney like the ones she so admired at the firm. For now, she would do her part as a paralegal.

Her backpack full, she zipped it up and turned off her desk light. She straightened the papers so she could stay organized.

"Emory, are you still here? Don't you have some big plans for this weekend? You need to get home."

"Oh, you startled me, Mr. Jones. Yes, I do, and I'm just leaving. By the way, congratulations on your bid to run for state senate this year."

"Thanks, and call me Max. I think we need to fight our battles on more than just the judicial front. We need to start making laws to protect the rights of every person. The government has no right to deny citizens' rights to people based on whom they love and how they identify themselves."

"Absolutely, and I hope we can help this couple in our case. Being denied the right to be joined legally in a civil union just because they are gay is just wrong and hateful. I don't understand how people use the Bible to persecute us. I hope one day we can change all of that, and everyone will see that love conquers all the lies. More than anything, I want to be a strong advocate for the injustice being done every day to all people who identify as gay or lesbian."

"We need more people like you, Emory. It will be a long, hard fight, but we will never give up. Fortunately, things are changing. Very soon, I believe we are going to turn the corner from tolerance to acceptance. My goal, if I'm elected, is to one day make sexual orientation a protected class. That is the only way to preserve our civil rights."

"I hope you succeed, and I will do all I can to help. Hey, you were right about my weekend. I guess I better head home. See you on Monday, and thank you for giving me this opportunity."

"You bet, Emory. Be safe and love the one you are with."

Emory laughed, "Oh, I will."

The drive to the condo was longer than she would have liked, but when they had looked at the place, they both felt it was home. She got in the Citation she was still driving and headed east. Tired but excited about the weekend, she mashed the gas pedal to move the old car along.

Reaching the condo, she pulled into her assigned parking place and walked quickly to the door. She entered their place and appreciated being home, especially tonight.

"I'm home, Kell. Where are you?"

"I'm in the kitchen. Come on in."

"Yum, that smells terrific, and you look great."

"And you are late. Don't think you can sweet-talk your way out of it."

Emory walked over and hugged Kelly, "I mean every word. What ya' making?"

"Only your favorite, chicken enchiladas and all the trimmings. I also made some mock sunrises."

"I feel spoiled."

"You are spoiled. Go change into some comfy clothes, and dinner will be ready when you are."

"Okay." Emory walked through the condo, humming as she went. They had only moved here a couple of months ago, and not all of the boxes were unpacked, but the decor they did have was tasteful and upbeat. Seeing a picture of her family with the twins who were growing so rapidly, she picked it up and rubbed her hand over it. "Love you, kids. Wish I could see more of you," she said to no one.

A twinge of sorrow and longing lingered as she put the photo back and changed clothes. She went to the dining room and saw a beautiful setting, complete with candlelight and music. Kelly brought two plates of food to the table and set them down and then poured the drinks.

"Enough already, Kelly. Sit down, will you?"

"I was just getting ready to. Now, do you care for a toast?"

"Would love one."

"To you, Emory. I can't believe we met seven years ago. I know it took a while for us to get together but happy fourth anniversary!"

Emory clinked her glass against Kelly's. "I am sure you are well aware that if I had my way, this would be our seventh anniversary. You know, Kelly, I liked you from the first minute we met—boy, that was romantic, wasn't it?"

"Yeah, in a frat house with a bunch of creepy guys. And you know, I fell for you, too, but I couldn't see us trying to be together then. I was coming out of a relationship from which I had been dumped. And you were coming out of a place of depression and confusion. You deserved to have time to explore, to try to find your footing."

"Well, thanks for letting me explore. I found out a hundred ways that girls can be screwed up. Let's see, there was the party girl, the dependent, the angry chick, the controller, the just-out-right crazy woman, and then, of course, the cheater. Yep, that was three great years. Oh, and I forgot Cat Lady; that was fun. Who has seven cats in a one-bedroom apartment? It was like walking into a giant kitty litter box."

"Oh, come on, Emory. It wasn't that bad."

"No, what was bad was knowing I wanted to be with you, but you kept me at arm's length."

"You know it was for your own good. I just could not pull you into the whole Peyton Place drama of me and the coach."

"Well, you have a point. If I had known that your prior girlfriend left you to be with Coach Day, it probably would have blown me away."

"And I couldn't risk having the coach take anything out on you just because of some crazy jealousy she might have dreamed up in her own head."

"All I know is that those three years when you gave me all those massages for my shoulder were pure torture for me."

"But they worked, didn't they—All-conference for two years and honorable mention as an All-American. The only reason you didn't make All-American is because State is such a small school, and a lot of politics goes into those selections."

"Kelly, Happy Anniversary." Emory pulled them back to the moment.

"You, too, babe. Really wish you could share the whole weekend with me."

"I do, too, Kell, but I can't let my family down, especially the twins."

"Just bad timing, I'd love to go with you, but I committed to Mary and Stacy and their big engagement party."

"Why does everything always happen at once? Give them my best and enjoy the party."

"Right back at you, beautiful. What time do you have to leave in the morning?"

"Probably around ten to get there by noon."

"Good, we can sleep in a little. Now take a bite and let me know how you like the anniversary dinner."

***

Josie finished the dinner dishes and watched Lee come in from trash detail. She loved that man more every day. He caught her staring at him and smiled sheepishly.

"What? What did I do?"

"You married me, had kids with me, and loved me for thirty-five years."

"Oh, is that all? I must be the man then, huh? What more can I do for my lady?"

"Well, since you asked..."

"When will I ever learn to keep my big mouth shut and quit while I'm ahead?"

"You are never ahead, Lee."

"True that."

"Can you get the folding table out and set it up in the living room. Then throw the tablecloth on and set the places for the kids. I think there will be ten of them in all. Grab the extra chairs and put them with the table."

"What about the decorations?"

"Oh yes, the streamers need to go around the table and overhead, and I guess we should go ahead and inflate the balloons. Oh, and the gifts, get them out of the closet and pile them in the corner. The other kids can add to the pile as they come in."

"Roger, I'm on it."

"I'll be in here putting the last touches on the cake and finishing up the snacks and party favors."

An hour later, Josie walked into the living room and marveled at Lee's decorating skills. "Lee, it looks wonderful. I didn't know you got blow-up animals, too."

"Yeah, I couldn't resist. They were just too cute."

"It's perfect. I know all the kids will enjoy it. Hard to believe Daniel and Hannah are already seven years old and starting school."

"Yep, time really does go by so fast. Hard to believe, too, that Emory has been gone for seven years."

"I am so happy she is coming home. I miss her so much. Ever since she graduated, we hardly ever see her. At least when she was in college, we could go to her games."

"Yeah, I miss her, too. She certainly did turn out to be some kind of basketball player, huh?"

"She really did. It's like college gave her a fresh start. Guess she was right about leaving early but letting her go when she was so young was one of the hardest things I've ever done," Josie sighed.

"I know, but she will be here tomorrow, and I'm really happy for the kids, too. Ever since they saw her play ball, they think she hung the moon. Sometimes I think she missed her calling. She has always been so good working with kids."

"I hope she is happy, Lee."

"She seems to be. I like her roommate, Kelly. She seems really nice."

"Yes, I like her, too, but I still worry about Emory sometimes."

"Josie honey, that is what mothers do—worry about their kids,"

"It's more than that, Lee. I just can't shake the feeling that she is adrift."

"Adrift?"

"I really can't put it into words. All I know is I pray for her every night. She has done very well for herself in school and now in a career, but there is something that's not right."

"If you feel so strongly about it, why haven't you told me this before?

"Because I can't even tell you now. I know none of this is making any sense to you, but I just can't figure out how to verbalize it."

"You think we ought to ask her if she wants to tell us anything?"

"You know how private she is, Lee. I don't think it would help. All we can do is love her and pray for her."

Chapter 24
Convicted

*A*fter an uneven night's sleep, Emory rose earlier than Kelly, showered, and made breakfast. Her mind was perplexed for reasons she could not understand. Always a sound sleeper, why couldn't she sleep last night? Whatever the reason, she just felt out of sorts and unsure of everything in her life.

Kelly finally walked to the kitchen and sat with her at the bar. They ate together and watched the squirrels as they acrobatically flew from tree to tree. After a reluctant goodbye, Emory got in Old Faithful and pointed the car toward home. For some reason, she was more excited about this trip home than she had been in years.

Uncharacteristically, she chose to listen to the radio rather than her cassettes. Flipping through stations brought more static than music. The clearest station was a man speaking, and after a futile effort to pick up anything else, she settled on it. His voice was clear and inviting and somehow seemed strangely alluring.

"Friends, I am so glad you have chosen to listen today. I have a message I want to go out to everyone. This is a delicate topic, so please know that this message is delivered in both love and truth."

"There is a great delusion in the minds and hearts of many today, and only the Holy Spirit can convict each person of the truth. The delusion I speak of is the gay Christian movement. Leaders and proponents of this movement have taken Scripture and manipulated, distorted, and twisted the words of God."

Emory shifted in her seat and reached to turn the station, no point in listening to another sermon on the shame and depravity of her life. Her reach was stopped short.

"Wait! Before you change stations, I want you who feel judged and shamed by others to know that God loves you and he is the only true judge. So please stay with me and just hear me out."

Emory drew her hand back from the radio, not fully knowing why. Something compelled her to listen even though she really did not want to hear what this man had to say.

"I wish I could sit down with each of you over a meal and just talk. What I would ask you to do is think about a few things. Many say that the Leviticus prohibitions against homosexuality are really talking about idolatry. Although I believe that the Bible is clearly talking about the specific sin of homosexuality, let's say that is true. But even if it is about idolatry, isn't that what a person does when he or she chooses to live for self instead of God? And isn't that what a person does when he or she chooses to live with and share a bed with someone of the same gender? When we choose our feelings over living in accordance with God's clear standard for our expression of sex, we are idolators.

"Here is the truth. We are all born with a sin nature that longs to be satisfied, and following the commandments of God just does not satisfy the appetites of the flesh. Can someone be both saved by God's grace and still live a life that continually violates God's expressed standard for sex? Let's be clear, God's standard is indisputable. The gift of sex was and is commanded by God in Genesis to be exclusively between only a man and a woman married to each other in covenant with God.

"So, can you be a gay Christian? The answer to that question is only known by each individual and our Creator, God. Only God knows our hearts, and only he is the true judge. But there are some strong indicators of salvation by the way a person lives out his or her life.

"Let's look at this question through the lens of his Word. God's number one commandment given to us through Moses is simple, 'You shall have no other gods before me.' Unlike earthly kings and rulers throughout the ages, with God, there will never be a co-regency that rules our hearts when we receive Christ as Lord and Savior. It is Christ and Christ alone. He will not allow anything to sully his holiness or compete for his glory.

"Jesus said in both Matthew and Luke that no one can serve two masters. Yes, the context there was about putting your faith and devotion in money above God. How much more that must be true when our bodies, the very temples of his Holy Spirit, are used to fulfill our fleshly desires above his will and desires for us. Jesus described the outcome of one who does try to serve both God and self. He said that person will hate the one and love the other or that he will be devoted to one and despise the other.

"This we do know with certainty: anyone who continues to habitually sin against God may not enter into heaven and definitely will not have the abundant life God promises his children. Be not deceived by the lie that no one is getting hurt by this sin. God may have a desire to use you in the lives of others, but due to disqualifying sin and disobedience, he cannot. We are living examples to others; to say we are Gay Christians is a confused identity that was never intended by our Creator. It falls far short of the holiness God desires for us.

"I want to speak now directly to those that are not true believers in Jesus Christ as Lord and Savior. You need, above all else, to come to a saving knowledge of Christ through his grace by faith. All you need to do is accept Him into your heart as the one and only master that you will follow at all cost. Make no mistake, friend, there will be a cost. It may cost you your job, your friends, and it will require sacrifice. But the rewards will far exceed the cost, and he will give you the power and grace you need to live your life in obedience to Him."

"Now, for those who have truly received Christ as Savior and are living a sinful, homosexual life, you need to have a long talk with Him. Sit down in a quiet place and read 1 John 3:9, where God tells us, 'No one who is born of God will continue to sin because God's seed remains in them; they cannot go on sinning because they have been born of God.' Then listen to the convictions of his Holy Spirit who lives within you. Is he truly Lord of your life?

"Listen, Christian, to be a disciple of Christ and receive his full blessings, Jesus says we must take up our cross and follow Him. What that means is that there will be appetites of the flesh we must reject, and, yes, we will suffer. Cutting away of the flesh always involves pain. But when we pick up our cross out of obedience to Him, that means our suffering will glorify Him. It means we make sure our relationship with Him is paramount. This morning, I would ask you again to let the Holy Spirit speak to you. Please respond to his promptings.

"Many say, 'But I was born this way, this is how God made me.' Friends, with tender love, I say to you that you have been deceived. God did not make anyone to be a sinner, but everyone in this fallen world is born with a sin nature. Did God make you gay? No. Were you born with a sin nature that can manifest itself as same-sex attractions? Yes.

"Could you do anything to keep from having these feelings? I believe the answer to that is probably not. Every gay person I have ever spoken to has told me they never chose to feel like this, but that is where the saving grace and power of his Spirit come in to give you freedom. This may or may not be freedom from the feelings and desires, but more important, he will always give you the freedom to overcome temptations that formerly held you in bondage."

"Now, I know I have covered a lot, but there is one more extremely important point I want to make. If you are convicted by the Holy Spirit and want with all your heart to change, know this, you cannot do it in your own strength. Your desire can be real and passionate, but only God can change your heart. So please do not try to do this in your own power. The failure you experience will only darken the place of despair you are currently experiencing. This process of change is what we call sanctification, and it can be a long, messy, and painful process. It is not uncommon to stumble and fall back into sinful ways during this time, but the Holy Spirit will never leave you, and he will constantly remind you that your identity is grounded in Christ alone."

"My friends, I pray that you will allow God to have his way in your life. This sinful practice of homosexuality is no worse than that of habitual lying and cheating, so do not let shame and fear keep you from confessing your sins first to God and then to a trusted believer. Good Christian counseling will go a long way in helping you in the journey out of this stronghold. Jesus came to set the captive free. If he is your Savior, he needs to be your Lord also. He longs to show his love to you. I pray for each of you. Remember, holiness cannot be hurried, and you must lean into the power of his patience and goodness.

"You have been listening to AK Ministries, a production of the Christian Counseling office of Aar..."

Barely aware of the tears rolling down her cheeks, Emory pulled to the side of the road, no longer hearing the radio. Her head on the steering wheel, she felt the full conviction of the Holy Spirit. Completely overwhelmed, she could hardly breathe as sobs of contrition flowed from her core. This was her moment when she must choose to either live by the light or in the darkness. "Self" had reigned in her heart for most of her life, even after her salvation. Yet, the realization of all that she would lose if she gave in to this conviction hit hard, trying to pull her back to partial obedience. Waves of grief over friends and even her job assaulted her mind and heart. The greatest sorrow of losing Kelly was devastating.

"My God, please, I love Kelly. This would crush her. Please don't make me leave her. I promised I would never hurt her."

A stirring in her soul silenced her pleas as a knowing of the answer came. *I love Kelly, too, my child, and I do not want to harm her either. Yet you both must know that your relationship with me is more important than with each other. It is not my desire that you should live together as you now do, and it is only if you stay that you will really hurt her."*

There was more. *How long, Emory, will you continue refusing complete surrender to me? And why do you participate in leading others away from me? I am not pleased when you perpetuate lies about my purity standards in your job and in your life. You are mine, and you are to make disciples of others, but instead, you lead them astray. Why do you continue to persecute me this way and grieve my Spirit that lives within you?*

Shaking and unable to reply, she simply sat with her head on the steering wheel and cried. Cars wheezed by; the radio played some songs, and time seemed eternal. Finally, she lifted her head and wiped away the tears.

Lord, you have been faithful to me all of my life even though I have sinned greatly against you. I tried to change once before, but you were not a part of that effort. This time, I know that it is only by your grace and the power of your Holy Spirit that you will change me. I put myself in your hands today. Lord, I need you so desperately. Thank you for opening my eyes today. I am so humbled in the presence of your holiness. Thank you for your mercy and your love. I love you, Lord, above all else.

The stirring within her continued. *Now go and confess your sins to your father and mother, and they shall give you the help that you will need. This will not be an easy change for you, and it will take time. It will require the full armor of Christ in this spiritual warfare. Put on the helmet of salvation to guard your mind and the breastplate of righteousness to protect your heart. Shod your feet with the readiness of the gospel of peace and tighten the belt of truth around your waist —the truth that your identity is in Christ alone. Finally, you need to pick up the shield of faith to quench the fiery darts of the evil one and your sword, which is the Word of God."*

***

The party was a smashing success. Daniel, Hannah, and all the kids played basketball with the one they looked up to, their own family hero, Emory. Josie's cake, along with a couple of gallons of homemade ice cream, were consumed faster than Lee could get the presents on the table.

Emory stood back for a moment and just watched the family and the fun. It had been longer than she could remember since she had really been here for them. Seventeen-year-old Emory would have been jealous and preoccupied. The twenty-five-year-old Emory of only a few hours ago would be going through the motions and trying to find a way to escape as quickly as possible—escape back to her life, not this one she did not share with her family. But all of that had changed, and now she was experiencing his goodness like never before.

She walked over to Eva and pulled her to the side. Eva was taken off guard but happy for Emory's show of family closeness.

"Eva, I need to ask you something."

"Sure, Emory, what is it? And before I forget to tell

you, thank you for being here. The kids adore you."

"Thanks, Eva, you know how much I love them. But I have to tell Mom and Dad something tonight that is going to be very hard for me to say and for them to hear. It will cause them pain and disappointment, and I just need some advice."

"Whatever I can do to help, you know I will."

"I can't really tell you what it is right now. They need to hear it first. I just wondered if you can tell me how they were with the problems you and Rick had early in your marriage. You know, how did they deal with everything?"

"Emory, I'm not sure anything you say could make them feel all the emotions they had toward Rick, but I want to assure you that there is nothing you could ever say that they will not forgive. They will move heaven and earth to help you with whatever it is. I promise you it will be more than okay. Listen, they have wanted you to open up to them for years now, but you never would."

"They what? You mean they know?"

"They know that ever since you lost Pepper, you have been hurting. They know something has changed you. Before you left for college, they were on the verge of just coming out and confronting you. Whatever it is, whatever your fears, they love you. Tell them, Emory, and get this burden off your back. We are your family, and we are here for you."

"Eva, I don't know what to say. I never thought any of you had the slightest idea that I was holding a dark secret."

"Emory, I haven't always been a good sister to you, especially when we were younger. I was so mean and ugly to you. You didn't do anything to deserve that.

I was just jealous and wanted you to stop infringing on my right to their attention. Emory, I've never told you I am sorry for that, so I am asking you now to forgive me."

"Eva, that was so long ago. I never even think about it. But of course, I forgive you. And thank you for your encouragement. Very soon, you will know too, okay?"

"Okay, now I know how much you don't like this, but I'm going to hug you now."

Emory rolled her eyes in mock protest, "No, you are not Eva."

"No?" Eva looked hurt.

"No, because I am going to hug you."

An hour later, the kids packed up and prepared to leave. Emory realized it was time to start preparing for one of the most critical conversations in her life with her parents. Now, thanks to Eva, she knew that it was all going to be okay. They had been waiting for years to listen to her.

Eva, Rick, and the kids loaded the car with birthday presents and said their goodbyes. The twins simultaneously dragged Emory down to their level and gave her bear hugs. After a five-minute wrestling match, Daniel and Hannah reluctantly gave in to Rick's commands and kissed Emory goodbye.

Eva gave Emory one last knowing look and winked. "You can do it," she mouthed and grabbed the nearest kid by the hand.

The door behind them closed, but the door before Emory was just beginning to open. She looked at Josie, already starting to clean up, then at Lee slouching on the couch.

"Whew," he said. "What a blowout. You did great,

Josie."

"You, too, Lee, and Emory, you were the absolute life of the party. All the kids just idolize you. We are so happy you came."

"I am happy, too, Mom, happier than you know. Uh, Mom, can you stop cleaning up for a minute and come sit on the couch with Dad."

Josie looked at Emory then at Lee. "Sure, honey."

Emory walked to the chair opposite the couch and brought it closer. Years of living her secret life were about to end, and the love of God was taking up residence. The fear and shame that had imprisoned her for so many years held no power over her now, for she knew that greater was he that was within her than he that is in the world.

"I want to tell you something about me that may shock and upset you, but please just let me say everything I need to get out without interruption. I am a sinner, saved by grace through faith, and today I really understand what that means."

Chapter 25
Triumph of Truth

*J*osie put away her mop and joined Lee on the couch. He reached over and put his arm around Josie, and they both looked at Emory. She sat down and cleared her throat. Unsure of how to begin, she prayed for the Holy Spirit to give her courage.

Seconds expanded to hours in her perception. Her parents sat patiently waiting, neither saying a word. She breathed deeply and looked at them in unabashed love and gratitude that God had chosen these two people to be her parents.

"Mom, Dad ..." she stammered.

Expecting one of them to say something, their silence strangely helped her regain equilibrium.

"As I know you remember, just before the twins were born, I had told you I needed to talk to you. Later, I told you I had wanted to talk to you about going to college early. That was a lie. There was something much darker that I wanted to tell you."

"Emory," Josie spoke softly, "we know you have been burdened with something for a long time. Whatever it is, you have to know we are here for you."

The dam broke and emotions gripped her throat and heart. "Oh, Mom, I am just so ashamed."

Lee leaned forward and gently spoke to his youngest daughter, "Emory, let me tell you something about shame you may not understand. Shame is an instrument of Satan himself. Shame makes us dig the hole we are in even deeper, so the darkness becomes even darker. Shame is a hostage-taker, a vile and evil one at that. It will steal your joy, your future, and your identity. The only way to overcome it is to expose it to the light of love, God's love.

"When Jesus hung on the cross, the Bible says he 'scorned the shame' that mankind had heaped upon Him as he became our sin offering. Scorning the shame means that he took shame and threw it back on itself so that it would no longer have the right or the audacity to try to stop Him. He took the very tool of Satan and said, 'Here, Satan, you know shame now because my children will know no shame in me.'"

"Emory," Lee looked into her eyes and smiled, "today you scorn that shame. You say yes to the Spirit of God that is within you. The only way to overcome shame is to expose it and claim the power of the cross. Do not be ashamed of the gospel that you know so well."

"Daddy, Momma, I, I have spent the last ten years living a lie. I have been so deceived and in the grips of this stronghold, this sin. Oh, this is so hard to say out loud to you."

"We are not given a spirit of timidity, Emory, but of power and of love and a sound mind. Go ahead, dear," Josie encouraged.

"Shane and Kelly—they have been more than friends to me. Shane was my first girlfriend, and Kelly and I are a couple right now. I have been living as a lesbian for years, and there are other girls you don't know about when I was in college. But on the way here today, the Holy Spirit convicted me, and I don't want to live that way anymore. I want to obey God and please Him. I never ever wanted to be attracted to women, and I am going to need some help to work through all of this."

With those words, an incredible warmth filled her heart; the darkness of a thousand nights of disobedience was chased away by a divine light. Hope was restored. The winter had passed to spring in an instant.

She looked up as both her parents rose and came to her and enveloped her in loving arms. They wept together, then laughed, then wept again. In unison and solidarity, they dropped to their knees as Lee led them in praise and glory for Emory's freedom.

"Lord of all, how do we begin to thank you for your power over sin? We glorify you, Lord, for you and you alone can break the chains of sin. We know that your goodness pursues us; your love compels us; your Son has saved us. We celebrate your victory, and we look for your continued guidance to walk with you closer every day. In Jesus' name, we pray. Amen."

"Emory, thank you for telling us. Thank you for trusting us, and, even more, for trusting in the Lord. We want you to know that we understand the courage it took for you to tell us, and we know that the Holy Spirit has done what none of us could ever do. Healing from all the hurts and wounds you have endured will take time, and we will be by your side every step of the way. I know a great Christian counselor that we can go to see. Would you be willing to do that?"

"Dad, I need help. I've tried to do this on my own, and that is just a fool's errand. It won't be easy, but, yes, I definitely want to see a counselor."

"We are doing this as a family because we have all been hurting. Do you want to tell Eva?"

"Eva has an idea, and I've already promised her I would tell her the secret. She is the one who encouraged me to talk to you tonight."

"Really?" Josie could not disguise her surprise.

Her face still wet with tears, Emory burst into laughter, "I know, Eva and I sharing a confidence— pretty miraculous, right? After all these years, we are finally discovering what sisterhood is all about."

Josie pulled Emory back into her arms. "Emory, my little girl, welcome back home."

Chapter 26
Aaron & Caleb

One month later

*E*mory opened her eyes to another new morning. Never had she known such sheer joy in watching the sun rise over the hill where she still gazed at Pepper's final resting place. Yet with all the joy, she knew the struggle was still very much a part of her life, and the battle would not be easy. She got up and walked to her bathroom to splash some water on her face.

Grabbing her prayer journal, she returned to her bed and plopped down. The entries started from the night she had told her parents about her wayward life of so many years. Rereading it, she once again wept.

Lord, I thank you for your grace and your goodness that has followed me all the days of my life. I truly know that you are God, and it is you who has made me. I am yours, and you will always fight for me.

Thank you, heavenly Father, for my earthly parents. Thank you that as shocked and hurt they were, they never for a moment stopped loving me. Thank you for my dad, who is searching for a good counselor to help me in my walk with you. Thank you, too, for your truth revealed that my mom has never rejected me but loves me without condition. And thank you for the reconciliation you are bringing with my family, es-

pecially Eva, and for the restoration of all you want me to be.

The post she had entered a week later had been one of the most difficult she had ever written. *Today I went back to tell Kelly that I could no longer be with her. My heart feels like it will never beat right again. We shared so much, laughed so much, and learned so much from each other. Lord, I pray for her and for me to give us strength to make all the arrangements necessary with our shared possessions and condo. I pray for your light of truth in her life. She is an amazing person who truly loves you but is still deceived by those that twist and distort your Word. Teach her by your Holy Spirit to see her sexuality through the truth of your Word and not to interpret your Word through the filter of her own feelings.*

Sighing deeply, she closed the journal and glanced at the clock. Already eight, she realized she needed to start getting ready. This was to be a big day, the first step in her counseling. Getting up from the bed, she started toward the shower when someone knocked on her door.

Laughing to herself, she answered, "I know, Dad, my appointment is at nine. Don't worry. I will be on time."

"It's not Dad. Well, he and mom are here, too, but it's me, Eva. We have a surprise for you. Hurry, it can't wait much longer."

Opening the door, she replied, "What on earth are you guys up to?"

The answer came roaring in, almost knocking her down. Kneeling, she was lavished with kisses all over her face.

"You are kidding me. You guys got me a dog? Seri-

224

ously? He is so cute. I love him."

The tan and white mass of fur snuggled up against her and relished her attention. He rolled over and used his paw to encourage a belly rub from Emory. Emory rubbed his underside and talked to him, "What a good boy you are. What's your name, boy?"

Eva answered, "His name is Salty. Honest, that was the name already given to him when we got him from the shelter. He is about a year old, and he really needs a good home."

"I can't believe it! Salty? Really?"

"Yes, the name sealed the deal. We all agreed," Josie replied.

Lee leaned down next to them and began to join Emory in petting him. "Emory, we want you to know that you are welcome to live here with us for as long as you want. We love having you here, but we also know that at some point, you are going to want to be out on your own. We thought that when you do move, Salty would make a great roommate for you."

"You all are so ...." She couldn't finish her words as the tears came and choked her voice.

Eva stepped in to rescue her. "Emory, no crying in front of the D-O-G. They are like kids. They pick up on everything."

Emory took a deep breath, determined not to laugh, but couldn't help herself. "Eva, stop it!"

True to form, Lee got everyone back on schedule. "Hey girls, we have some important business to take care of today. Emory, your mom and I are going to meet with Aaron first. Then you come on over and be there by nine. Josie, we need to go. Salty can stay here with you while you get ready. Then bring him down, and Eva will dog sit until you get back.

We don't want any accidents with a new dog in the house."

"Okay, and thank you all so much. My new furry blessing is wonderful. I'll be there. See you soon. Love you."

***

A little before nine, Emory parked her car and looked up at the four-story building. She opened the front door to the lobby and saw a large directory on the wall by the elevator. Finding the name "Aaron Knox," she traced her finger across the ledger to find the accompanying suite and room number. Her nerves were intensified when she realized the location was faded beyond legibility.

"Oh no, what do I do now?"

"Excuse me, can I help you find where you need to go?"

She turned and saw a tall man standing behind her. He had dark hair and the kindest eyes she had ever seen. He looked like an athlete and was probably her age or a little older.

"Yes, I could definitely use some directions. I am looking for a Christian counselor. His name is Aaron Knox."

The young man smiled, and his periwinkle eyes seemed to become even kinder. "That is just where I am heading! His office is on the second floor. Shall we take the elevator or stairs?"

"I'd prefer stairs—work off some of the anxiety." *Why on earth had she volunteered that little nugget?*

He laughed and pointed her toward the stairs. As they walked, he started up a conversation that she had unexpectedly invited. "I am actually filling in for

Mr. Knox's assistant this week. Being nervous is not a bad thing. If you weren't, there would probably be no reason to see a counselor."

"Thank you for that. It makes me feel a little better."

"But not much, and that is okay. You will be fine once you meet Mr. Knox. He is a good guy, really easy to talk with. My name is Caleb, by the way, and let's see if I can remember; you must be Emory, right?"

"Yes, I am Emory Johnson."

"Don't worry. I haven't been doing surveillance on you. I saw your name on the appointment calendar. I think I met your parents a little while ago."

"Yes, they came earlier."

Turning the corner, they stopped at Room 116, and Caleb opened the door. The waiting room was empty except for the attractive chairs and wall decor. Caleb went to a closed door and knocked softly. "Emory is here."

The door opened, and Emory was relieved to see her parents smiling at her.

Next to them stood a man about her dad's age. He was well built and well-mannered.

"Hi, Emory. I've just been talking to your folks about you, and I am so very happy to meet you. You know, your dad and I go way back. I knew him before you were born."

Emory shook his extended hand. She could not shake a feeling of familiarity. What was it about him she somehow knew? It was not his appearance; it was... his voice. She knew she had heard it before and not that long ago.

"Nice to meet you, Mr. Knox." She shook his outstretched hand.

"And I see you have already met my son, Caleb."
"Your son? Why didn't you tell me?"

"Didn't want to make you even more nervous, Emory."

"Yes," Aaron continued, "Caleb has just completed seminary. I told him he may be a graduate and a smart guy, but he still has a lot to learn. So, I've got him helping me out to pick up some pearls of wisdom."

Caleb laughed, "Okay, Dad, enough about me. I will leave you all alone to get on with everything you need to discuss."

"Wait, Caleb," Lee said. "We will walk with you. We'll see you at home, honey. We love you. Aaron is a good friend and a great counselor. I really think he will help us all."

"Okay, bye, Dad, Mom. Pet Salty for me."

"We will. Love you."

"Love you, too."

When the door closed, Emory broke into a cold sweat. Despite all of the support and encouragement, she suddenly felt trapped. She wasn't ready for any of this. To talk about something so private, so depraved, with a perfect stranger was just too much. She wanted desperately to turn and run, but then she heard that voice again."

"Emory, please sit wherever you like. Can I get you something to drink?

She moved to a nearby chair and slowly lowered herself into it. "Uh no, no thank you. I am fine. Can I ask you something?"

"Anything."

"Have we met before? You just seem, so, well, like I know you."

"No, I don't think so, but I am glad you feel that way. I want you to feel completely free to be yourself. There is no need to cover up what you really think or feel in this office. This is a safe and confidential place."

"Okay."

"Today, let's just get to know each other. Your dad tells me you are quite the basketball player. Honorable mention All-American at State, I hear?"

"My dad brags about me a little more than he should sometimes."

"All dads do that, Emory. For example, my son Caleb, as you know, just graduated from seminary. He was also a standout basketball player at West Virginia. He even got drafted to the pros but decided that wasn't what the Lord had in store for him.

"Really, that was a bold decision."

"Yep, but I think he is following his true calling. I do think he would have made it in the pros. He is one of the purest shooters you will ever find, but he left the possibilities of fame and riches to follow the Lord. Now we are just waiting to see exactly what ministry he will pursue."

"That's quite a sacrifice."

In the world view, it certainly is, but when you know that everything we have really belongs to God, it's no sacrifice at all. It's obedience that provides joy unspeakable."

Emory found herself very much at ease in a short period of time. Their hour together went by quickly, and she almost didn't want it to end. A knock at the door was their signal to stop.

"Dad, I hate to interrupt you and Emory, but we need to tape your program for this week's broadcast,"

Caleb called from behind the door.

"It's okay, son, come on in."

Entering the room, Caleb addressed Emory first. "So, was I right? He's a pretty good guy, isn't he?"

Emory laughed, "Yes, you were right. You are pretty blessed to have a dad like him. Can I ask what this broadcast is you talked about? I may want to listen to it sometime?"

Caleb smiled, "Sure. It comes on Saturday mornings at ten o'clock and is aired across the state. It's called 'AK Ministries,' AK, of course, being Aaron King."

"Caleb is the producer, and he is usually the one who comes up with the topics. I think he is more in tune to the hot topic these days than I am. It's just what happens when you get old," Aaron laughed.

Emory snapped her fingers and looked excitedly at Aaron. "That's it. That is why your voice is so familiar to me. Aaron, you are a large part of the reason I am on the road to restored hope and healing. A month ago, I was on my way home to visit with Mom and Dad. I accidentally—or rather providentially—tuned into your program about breaking the bonds of homosexuality. The Holy Spirit did the rest."

Suddenly, Emory drew in her breath in fear and panic. She had just told Caleb why she was there, and she was petrified. What would he think? And why did it matter so much to her?

Seeing the worry in her eyes, Caleb smiled. "God is for you, Emory, and so are we. Don't ever let Satan choose your identity or stifle your voice. I was the one who selected that topic because my best friend in college struggled with same-sex attractions. There are so few places to go for help, and I didn't know

230

or understand exactly what he was going through. I just want him and you to know you are loved and you are not alone in your fight. Thank you for your courage, and if you ever need support, I am here for you, too. Dad is your counselor; I am your friend."

Relieved beyond description, Emory breathed again. "Caleb, I've never met anyone like you or your father. See you next week, Aaron, and maybe you, too, Caleb?"

"I really hope so, Emory."

Was he flirting with her, or did she just want him to be? What a novel desire.

Chapter 27
Crisis of Belief

Six months later, 26-year-old Emory

$\mathcal{E}$mory walked up the now-familiar steps to the office she was growing to love. As had been the case for weeks now, she found herself hoping that Caleb would be there. He was indeed her friend, but was it something more? Could it really be possible that she was attracted to him in the same way she had always been before to women?

Pushing the door open, she was disappointed to see only the assistant there, no Caleb. But that was short-lived as she heard the jovial whistling of her—well, whatever he was to her. One thing was certain, she thought of him constantly and loved being with him.

"Hey, Emory, good to see you today. You look great."

"Thanks, Caleb. Working hard?'

"Just trying to decide what topic to cover in the broadcast today. I really like doing these programs, you know."

"Maybe one day you will have your own on-air program."

"I never thought about it before, but maybe you are right. That is if I can fit it in with my other job.

"You have another job?"

"As of tomorrow, yes. Your dad asked me to be the new director of the Teen Center, and I accepted."

"What? Wow, that is great. The job suits you perfectly, but why didn't Dad tell me?"

"I asked him not to so I could. Just wanted to see the look on your face. It was a good call on my part. I love to see you smile."

"I seem to do most of my smiling when I am with you."

"Yeah? Good, I like that. How is your new job going, by the way?

"Oh, I absolutely love it. I am still a little nervous. Teaching middle school kids is tough enough, but learning the rules and all the personnel is not easy either. I'm also coaching the girls' basketball team, and I am super nervous about that and dealing with disgruntled parents."

"You will do great. It's your heart to teach and coach. Hey, you want to go over to the Teen Center with me after you finish your session and shoot some hoops. I've got a couple of teenage boys we old folks need to take to school on the court. They challenged us to a two-on-two. Will you be my teammate?"

"I relish the thought of showing those boys up. A little humility will do them good. As for being your teammate, I'd be honored."

"They have no idea what's in store for them," he laughed. "Then maybe afterward we could get a bite to eat?"

"Sure," Emory replied unsteadily. *They had never eaten out together. Was this a date?* "That sounds like fun." She smiled to hide her uncertainty.

"Great, I'll see you later. Have a good session with Dad."

Fighting to regain her equilibrium, she walked past the assistant toward the door to Aaron's office. Suddenly, the exterior door opened, and a delivery girl walked in, almost running into Emory. She was young and smiled at Emory, "I'm so sorry for startling you."

"It's okay," Emory stammered and was staggered by the thoughts that flooded her mind. *You can run into me anytime. I've never seen anyone so beautiful. Wonder if you would go out and have coffee with me."*

"Say, I think I know you," the girl continued. "Aren't you Emory Johnson? I used to watch you play ball at State. Wow, you were great. I was still in high school, but I modeled my game after you."

Emory's heart skipped a beat, and her attraction grew. "Yes, that was me."

"Emory, are you ready?" Aaron stood at his opened door to call her in.

Not now, Aaron. Wait, no, that's not the right thought. I should say thank you for rescuing me, Aaron, but this girl, I really like her. It wouldn't hurt to get her number, would it? No, no, no!"

"Yes, Doctor Knox." She walked into his office as he closed the door.

"Doctor Knox? Where did that come from? It's Aaron, remember?"

"Yes, of course, I'm sorry. Guess I'm a little preoccupied today."

"Oh, something bothering you?"

She hesitated. Up until this very moment, she had been completely honest with him. He had made it very clear from the beginning that holding anything back would just impede her progress. He called it the "foundational rule."

235

Her thoughts lifted her away from Aaron. *This thing with Caleb, it seems so personal, and maybe it is just in my imagination. How embarrassing it would be to say something and then find out Caleb only wanted to be my friend. And how* could she *ever admit her feelings for both Caleb and the delivery girl? None of it made sense. Am I just too broken to ever fix? Too crooked to straighten?*

"Emory, I can see you are having a conversation in your mind with yourself. If you are conflicted about anything, you must not cover it up or ignore it. You need to name it and face it with authority."

Suddenly a new swirl of unwelcomed thoughts filled her mind. *Remember that beautiful girl who complimented you? Remember how attracted you were to her just minutes ago? What makes you think you can ever change? Why don't you just do what comes naturally to you? Why fight against yourself, against who you truly are? These conversations are not helping. Your same-sex attractions are still there because this is who you are. You are gay whether you want to admit it or not. Either accept that or admit you are going to be miserable all of your life.*

"Emory, are you okay? You are deathly white. Listen, you don't have to say a word. Come and sit down and just breathe deeply. No pressure. Just relax and tell me what we are going to do today."

She followed his instructions, and gradually the spinning in her head subsided but not the threats and warnings. She finally focused on Aaron and tried, a futile effort, to give him a half-smile. She knew he would not be fooled.

"Could I have some water, please?" She bought time trying to come up with a story that would conceal her true feelings. His caring eyes were fixed on her. He had earned her trust long ago, but fear and confusion pulled her away from disclosure.

Finally, he broke the silence. "Emory, maybe it would be helpful if we prayed. Would that be okay with you?"

She gave a mute affirmation by nodding and bowing her head. Closing her eyes, she wanted desperately to be rid of the confusion and chaos of thoughts and emotions. Feeling a hand on her shoulder took her through a flood of memories: Pepper, Shane, basketball, Kelly. The turbulence increased. Would she ever find the peace her Lord promised?

"Father, we come into your presence to praise your name and give you glory. You know our hurts and wounds. You know our innermost secrets and the depravity in our hearts, and yet you love us anyway. We claim the victory that Jesus died on a cross to give us. In our struggle, Lord, we discover how weak and ineffective we are, and we lean on your Word, your Holy Spirit, your promises. Remind us, Father, to take every thought captive and give it to you. We need you, Lord. With every temptation that we resist, may this be our act of worship unto you. You have given us the command to fear not, so we give to you any spirit of fear that is trying to invade our lives. In Jesus' name, we pray. Amen."

"Amen," Emory echoed. She looked up and met his eyes. This time her smile was genuine, and she knew the power of the Spirit would give her a way to voice all the things she had desperately wanted to hide.

"Aaron, I am just so confused. For the first time since I have been coming to see you, I have been attracted to a girl, actually that girl outside your office. I thought I was past it. It's so bizarre, especially because I think I am starting to have feelings for," she hesitated only for a moment, "for Caleb."

"That would be confusing, but that is just what the enemy wants. If you are confused, you lose your focus on Jesus. First, do not allow yourself to think you are failing in your efforts of restoration. The hurts and pain in your life have deep, deep roots. Reverting back to the comfort you found in same-sex attraction is natural. You are defaulting to what you know will give you a sense of security, but you have already taken the most important step by exposing your feelings to the light."

"The next thing you want to do is claim victory and make the thought that wanted to enslave you a prisoner of yours. You have the control. You have the victory. Your unwanted thoughts and feelings do not."

Aaron continued, "It is important, too, that we try to understand what triggered your default reaction. I think I can help you with that."

"Good, because I was just going through the day, and then right before I came in here, I was waylaid."

"Most of the time, when we revert to things that bring us comfort even though we don't want them, we give in to them anyway because of some stress or crisis in our life. It could be something new we are facing, something that triggers our insecurity. For you, it's pretty easy to see, you are in a new job. You're getting ready to move out on your own from your parents' house, and then there is Caleb—something completely new."

Emory blinked and recognized the truth in everything Aaron was saying. "You are so right! All of this, especially Caleb, is so new. It's exciting but scary too. I feel so uneasy and anxious because I don't even know if he feels anything for me."

Aaron leaned in and looked her square in the eyes, "it is not my place to speak for my son, Emory, but he does talk about you all of the time. He is very fond of you. All you need to do is just listen to the wisdom of the Spirit and believe that all things are possible in Christ."

"Yes, all things are possible. Thanks, Aaron. Is it okay with you if we end our session a little early today?"

"Early? Well, yes, if that is what you want. But, Emory, you are not running from anything, are you?'

"No, not at all. More like maybe running to something. Caleb and I are going to the Teen Center and then out to eat."

Aaron smiled. "So why are you still sitting here?" He squeezed her hand and walked her to the door. They walked out directly into Caleb's path.

"Finished?" he asked expectantly.

"Just getting started," Emory said.

"What?"

"Never mind, son, you two have a good time. See you next week, Emory."

Chapter 28
Spiritual Warfare

"Hi, Aaron, good to see you," Emory said as she walked into his office. "I want to thank you again for last week. It really helped me when you cut through all that confusion about, you know, everything."

"Glad we could talk through it. So you have had a good week?"

"Yes, a very good week."

"I'm happy to hear that. Ready for a full session today? This one might be a little tough but rewarding."

"You sound like me when I put my team through a two-hour practice."

"And are they better for it?"

"I see where you are going. Yes, let's get started."

"Emory, now that you have told me your full story, I just want to again thank you for being willing to be so open with me. I have spent a lot of time going over all my notes, and today I want to begin to try really to flush out the underlying causes for your same-sex attractions based on your history."

"That does sound a little intimidating to me."

"I think you will find it can be a little painful but very illuminating. Do you think you are up for it?

"Pain is how we grow, and light is good. Let's do it."

"Looking at your childhood, first, you were born prematurely. The expected boy was you, a girl, and your older sister was very jealous and taunted you because of your tomboy propensities. When you were only four, your mother took you to a babysitter instead of staying home with you. You and your mother never had a lot of things in common, so she spent most of her time with your sister, Eva, who kept telling you she was loved more than you."

"You're right on the money, Aaron."

"Good. Listen closely to this, Emory. Children are excellent observers but very poor interpreters. When you observed all of these things, your interpretation as a child was 'my mom rejects me. She did not want me in her womb, so I was born early. I disappointed my parents and sister by not being a boy. I like doing things that boys like. My mother never could grow to love me, so she sent me to a sitter and went to be with other kids and spent all her time with Eva, the daughter she did love.'"

He continued, "As an adult, I think you can see how flawed those interpretations were, but young Emory was deeply wounded by the rejection she perceived."

Emory studied the design on the picture frame behind Aaron, trying to bring into focus everything he had said. Processing this was not easy, but it lingered in her mind. Was she really as deeply hurt and damaged as Aaron said she was?

"So now, let's move on to Emory at age eleven. You received Jesus as your Savior and had a divine revelation in your dream that Satan was going to "sift" you. My dear one, that is one of the most incredible dreams I have ever heard. Doubtless you had the joy of salvation, but there was a dark cloud over you. Instinctively, you knew it was evil, but Satan used the spirit of fear to prevent you from telling anyone about the prophecy of your sifting.

"Here is a key point I want to give you. Satan hates humanity because God loves us. This is the crux of what we call "spiritual warfare." You see, when each of us is born, we are on Satan's radar. That means he is going to watch and wait to find out where our weak spots are. If our temperaments and genetics make us prone to gambling, that is where he will direct his temptation. If we are prone to anger, he will feed that weakness. No matter what the individual's weakness is, he will find out. He cannot read minds. Only God can do that, but he can observe and plant his thoughts into minds. His goal, as Jesus said in John 10:10, is to 'steal, kill, and destroy' us.

"When you were saved at age eleven, you were no longer just on his radar screen; you were in his crosshairs. I believe that God's original intention for your life was for you to be used in a great way to bring him glory. Because of that, Satan intensified his relentless attacks.

Emory's head swam. *Spiritual warfare? In Satan's crosshairs? Attacks?*

"Aaron, this is all so, I don't know, out there. I need some time to process these concepts."

"I completely understand, Emory. I'm going to give you some Bible verses to read, and you take all the time you need. What we are talking about here is something that most preachers are afraid to speak about, and certainly, most laypeople have never even considered the possibility. But Emory, this is not some fantasy that religious fanatics throw out there. It is real—Satan, demons, angels—it is all real.

"Let me leave that for now and move into your

teens and twenties. You carry with you even to this day the hurt and brokenness of your childhood. To assuage that hollowness in your soul, you needed to find someone to love you. Let me put one concept to rest. God never intended for you to be gay. He did not make you that way as so many of the pro-gay advocates preach, but he knew exactly how Satan tried to hurt you. Because he can see the beginning from the end, he knew you would be sitting in my office today, seeking his will. You did not choose to have these feelings. You discovered they were there. Yes, the feelings are a part of you, but a part that is broken and in need of the healing touch of Jesus. You did not want these feelings any more than you wanted to be hurt, but your feelings of rejection and hurt are how you discovered them.

"Other people may develop same sex attractions for different reasons. Every person has his or her own unique set of circumstances and responses. But I hope now you are beginning to come to an understanding of your same sex-attractions and know you have the power to defeat them and be made whole again.

"You may be wondering what triggered or accelerated your discovery in your childhood. Well, Lynn, your youth director, was the first attraction you experienced, and you may not have even known what was going on. All you knew was she made the hurt go away by accepting you and encouraging you. She was the woman you wanted to be, and you felt drawn to her because she represented security and confidence to you.

"Now, I move to the last point. What was it that moved your attractions from the mind and heart to acting on them with the body? What was the catalyst that moved you to your first physical relationship? It is common that when there is a crisis of some sort and your stress level is increased, temptations get the strongest foothold. When Pepper died and Shane was there, it was Satan's perfect storm of deceit, and the desires of the flesh were no longer controllable in your own strength. Yes, the Holy Spirit is more powerful than Satan, but you lacked the knowledge, the discipleship, to cry out for help.

"As you soon found out, trying in your own strength to overcome the stronghold is always futile. Satan continued to tempt you. When you were away at college and no longer close to parents and the truth of God's church, Satan used the world's theology to cement the theft of your identity—or so he thought.

"Okay, Emory, I've done a lot of talking. What questions or comments do you have?"

"I am overwhelmed. Sometimes the light is blinding, and I think this is one of those times but in a good way. The parts of what you have said that I understand are amazingly liberating, but there is still so much that is just a blur. It eludes my comprehension right now. But I do not reject any of it because something inside me gives me a sense of truth in it all."

"That is a great answer and approach to all of this. Look, I know you are exhausted after this session. This has been a full-throttle fire hose of information I have flooded you with today. Go home. Get some rest. Pray, and read the Word. It will come. It's hard work, but it will come. Remember, the Holy Spirit is your teacher, not me."

"Thank you, Aaron, thank you."

Chapter 29
Gabriel's Revelations

*E*mory barely made it home without falling asleep at the wheel. It was only mid-afternoon, but a nap was beckoning. She and Salty went upstairs, and she spread out on the bed with him. Sleep came immediately, but it was a fitful, dreamed-filled slumber.

She opened her eyes to a dream—again, divinely sent. She was standing in a field of dazzling colors and then saw a most glorious being. He held out his arms to her and spoke:

Emory, precious child of God, I am an angel of Yahweh, the divine name of the Lord God. My name is Gabriel. I was there when you were born, ensuring that your premature birth did not harm you, I was sent by God to preserve your life when Satan sent the car that killed your beloved Pepper, and I have been your guardian angel throughout your life. I witnessed the hand of Jesus permanently write your name in the Lamb's Book of Life. I have seen all that Satan has done to sift you. I have come now to help you understand.

Gabriel, why have I struggled so much with feelings I do not want?

Emory, do you remember when you received Jesus as your Savior?

Yes, Gabriel, like it was yesterday, I remember the

dream I had. At the end of that dream, I was told that God would allow Satan to sift me. What does that mean?

Sifting is a severe testing of your faith in God.

Is it these same-sex attractions that are my sifting?

Emory, you are a beloved child of God, and that enrages Satan. Satan sifts by tempting you to sin against God, and he tries to get you to choose to follow your own desires above God's. That is what Satan himself did, and you know the consequences.

Let me show you how Satan has tried to operate in your life even from the time when you were still in your mother's womb. Prepare yourself, for I now take you back to hear Satan's very words.

Hear me, my demons. I want to focus on what you have seen in this created world. Have you located anyone who is reaching out in love to others and giving all glory to the one who made them? Speak up, for nothing angers me more than these so-called faithful followers.

Ah, Demon Scout, I knew I could count on you. Tell me whom you have seen?

I have been watching Lee and Josie Johnson. They are very active and true in their church.

They sound like some pretty juicy prey to me, Demon Scout. What is their current status?

It appears that Josie just had another child. However, the baby has been born early and is a girl rather than the boy they had expected.

Babies are so precious to these kinds of believers; perhaps this baby shall be our attack point—a girl expected to be a boy, hmmm. Oh yes, I have a most diabolical plan. The Johnsons shall suffer for their faithfulness. I will send Demon Babel to confuse the child in her gender and Demon Scorner to heap shame upon her. This child will be corrupted in the vilest of ways in the eyes of the church, and she will seek comfort from those that spread my lies. I will ensure that the joy of this family will be stolen. In this case, it is the temperament and perceptions of this child that will be the place of vulnerability.

Emory asked, Gabriel, why, why would God let this happen?

God allowed Satan's temptations against you, but he did so to give you the opportunity to rise up and stand for Him. The difference is the intention. Satan intends to destroy your soul; God intends to give you victory. If you allow God to rule in your heart, the temptations become tests that will draw you closer to Him. The sifting acts to purify and make you stronger in your faith and in your walk with the Lord.

Emory, all of God's ways are not known or understood even by his angels, but let me assure you, he has always had me watching over you.

Thank you, Gabriel, for explaining all of this, but when I was eleven, I was saved. Why did everything start getting worse after that?

Emory, it is hard for you to understand how much Satan hates you, especially when you turned your life over to Jesus. He knew he was defeated, but that only made him intensify his attack against you because to hurt a child of God hurts God, too. Listen to Satan's fury.

Oh, my demons, how I hate Yahweh and his believers! It is true that this child Emory is now indwelt with the very Spirit of our enemy. She has a guarantee over her that we cannot touch, change, or distort. I detest his victory. I always have and always will.

It is now set that Emory will spend eternity in heaven with him. But how she will spend her time on earth is still a battle to be waged. I vow by all that I am, by all my power, that though she is saved, she will walk with me on earth.

Babel, you shall ensure that you use every form of temptation against her. You shall deceive her in every possible way. Kill what she loves and give her a desire for women rather than men. I have raised up an apostate church that will twist the will of the Creator in her mind, and she shall believe them.

Emory shook her head in disbelief. So Pepper? Satan tried to kill me then, too?

Yes, but I was guarding you; Yahweh knew every plan and scheme of Satan before they were even formed in his mind.

It was Satan's plan to use all of these things to tempt me, and I fell for it. I failed the Lord. I believed lies instead of his truth. Worse, I led others astray. I failed him for years and years; I wasted so much of my life.

Emory, Yahweh has sent me to remind you that you are forgiven and to tell you that he still desires to use you. He wants you to recall how his apostle, Peter, failed him, too, and yet he was forgiven. Much more, Jesus built his church on Peter. The denier became the proclaimer; the fearful became the faithful. You must keep your eyes on Jesus. Your past is a part of his plan. As he told Peter, he wants you to go and feed his sheep. He wants you to experience the joy of making disciples.

Yes, Gabriel. Yes, Lord, I will fulfill your desires for me.

I will, I will. Emory awakened, still repeating her

last words of the dream. Fully awake, she said again,
I will. I will follow you, Lord.

Salty rolled over and put his paw on Emory's
chest. Even he somehow wanted to be included in
the amazing love Emory now knew.

Chapter 30
Gratitude

1992, 28-years-old

Hard to believe that this was going to be the last time she parked in this lot, went into this building, climbed these stairs, and sat with Dr. Aaron for a counseling session. Where had the time gone? She felt like she had shed her old self completely. Like the Bible said, she was a new creation through the power of the Holy Spirit. Jesus truly had given her life to the fullest though she did not deserve it. How humbling it was to realize and fully know his grace and mercy.

She greeted the assistant who was on the phone but motioned her to go into the office. She opened the door and saw her counselor, her friend, and soon to be her father-in-law sitting at his desk.

"Emory, it's good to see you. How are you?"

"I'm so happy, Aaron, happier than I ever thought possible. I've been thinking about all the years I spent believing and living a terrible lie. You have walked with me through all the shame and guilt and confusion. And more than that, you have helped me understand that even those years have not been wasted. It took a while, but now I know that God uses everything, even our darkest moments, to draw us close to Him."

The words were powerful and touching. He smiled

and let her continue.

"Last night, I read Psalm 119:71: 'It was good for me to be afflicted for now I know his decrees.' If I had to write one sentence to describe my life, I think that would be it. The more I think about it, the greater the depth of its truth sinks in."

"Yes, the Word of God is an amazingly complex and profound book. What does that verse mean to you?"

"That's a hard question to put words together for an answer. I have been made better by these years of struggle. I feel like my relationship with Jesus is vibrant. My thirst for his Word is insatiable. My longing to tell others about him is consuming. My gratitude for his grace and forgiveness is inexpressible. My affliction has become the crucible of my abundant life in Him. By the power of the Holy Spirit, everything that tried to destroy my faith in God has led to a deeper desire to obey Him."

"Emory, you sound absolutely giddy when you speak of your afflictions. Do you realize what a completely different person you are now from the woman who first came to me a couple of years ago?"

"Incredible, isn't it? Truly knowing his decrees through experience nurtures me every day. That word *know* is *yada* in Hebrew. I looked it up. It means to have an absolute degree of certainty, of intimacy. And because I know his decrees, I treasure them, live by them, and keep them close to my mind and heart. It is so easy to be misled by everything this world offers, but those things are hollow. Jesus is solid and never changing. I desperately need him, and he desperately wants me never to forget that my identity is in Christ alone."

"Emory, I believe the student is teaching the teacher now. You have enriched my life, and I am so happy that our relationship is not ending. It is expanding."

"I can never thank you enough for everything. That radio program was the beginning of God's arm reaching out to bring me home. He never gave up on me. His goodness kept chasing after me. You and Caleb were the life preserver he tossed to me that day. Aaron?"

"Yes, Emory."

Tears rolled down her cheeks and stifled her words, but she persevered. "I love Caleb more than I ever thought possible. He is so kind and good to me. I will do everything I can to be a godly wife and life partner. Thank you for having such an amazing son. I am blessed with him and with my new daughter-in-law. I've been praying for you two and will do so as long as God gives me breath."

"Thank you, Aaron."

"I do have one request, and knowing Josie, I am not the first to make it."

Emory smiled knowingly, "Yes, we want to give you grandchildren soon."

"Great!"

Emory glanced at her watch. "Oh my goodness, it's almost one. Guess I better go. I'm meeting Eva and mom at the house to go over wedding plans. They have tried to hide it from me, but it is really a surprise bridal shower. Now don't ever tell them I knew. I've been practicing my 'Oh-what-a-surprise-I-didn't-have-a-clue' face."

Aaron laughed. "My lips are sealed."

"You know, we are only three weeks away. Caleb is not getting cold feet, is he?"

"I have seen my son perform under intense pressure many times. He was always as cool as a cucumber. But, Emory, my boy is so nervous and excited I'm just praying his adrenaline doesn't send him into a medical emergency. He is the happiest man on earth right now."

"I can hardly wait either. Sometimes I can't catch my breath. See you soon, Dad."

"I like the sound of that."

Chapter 31
Marriage and Mission

1994, 30-years-old

$\mathcal{A}$s I began this story, please allow me the privilege of drawing it to a close—though it will never truly end. I picked up my son, Caleb, and grandson, Josiah, at least twenty minutes before we needed to leave. Tonight was a very special night, and I wanted to get there early. Prying three-year-old Josiah away from his favorite playmate, Salty, had not helped to speed my plans. Caleb and I were both a little anxious. You will see why.

We dropped Josiah off at the sitter's, and I sped to our destination. We parked and walked in to take a seat close to the front. The crowd was large, and we were glad for that. I saw Lee with Josie and Eva with her family. We sat next to them.

The program opened with a praise team, too loud for this old man, but the kids loved it. Okay by me.

Then the leader came on stage for introductions, "Ladies and gentlemen, thank you for being here tonight. I am Bob West, executive director of *Delight in the Lord Ministries*. You are here for your own reasons. Some are strugglers; some are parents or friends of strugglers; some are pastors or lay ministers. Regardless of your personal status and motivation, above all else, I pray we are all here to serve and glorify our Lord Jesus Christ.

Our ministry is geared toward providing resources and guidance to help those who struggle with same-sex attraction and/or gender confusion. The theme of our conference this year is *Life to the Full.* I know of no better person to hit the keynote for that theme than our speaker, Mrs. Emory Grace Johnson Knox."

I listened to Emory that night with many emotions—all good. The overwhelming sense of her sheer joy captivated everyone there. I looked at her family and my son. All were crying. That is when I realized as she ended her presentation that I, too, was weeping and praising God. I'll let you listen to her closing:

"And so that is my testimony. After I told my parents, it took me years of struggle to break free from the stronghold of homosexuality. But I want to tell everyone who is struggling: 'Draw near to God, and he will draw near to you.'

"There are many who discount my story, thinking the real lie is that God can truly change a heart. Sadly, they are wrong but do not even know it. I know many who are like I was who have now been transformed by God. We are new creations, made so by the one and only Creator God.

"Everyone here needs to know that if we are completely his, our identity is in Christ alone, not in our feelings or our selfish desires. We must begin to spread the truth that homosexuality is a behavior that can be changed. It is not an identity,

"As I'm doing today, I speak to as many people as I can so that God's truth will be made known. Many say these efforts are futile, for how can I combat all the falsehoods and lies in the media and society? The point is just that: my efforts are futile without

God. But for God, there is no amount of opposition that will ever defeat him.

"Parents, please guard your children carefully. Talk with them. Listen to them and read them Bible stories. Surround them with love and teach them the truth. But be aware that sometimes, no matter what you do, children will make the wrong decisions. If you do have a prodigal child, do not blame yourself but continue in love and prayer. Never give up on them. In your love, make sure you never distort or dilute God's truth, for to condone their sin is the most harmful and unloving thing you could do.

"It is important, too, that I address the Church today. We, as believers, are not to judge but rather to love the sinner. But we are always to balance love with the truth of God's Word. There is no place for us to heap pharisaic shame upon those in the stronghold of sexual impurity. At the same time, we should give no allowance for the distortions and apostasy that some churches have embraced.

"God's standard for our sexuality is absolute, and to adjust, dilute, or pervert his standard is a sin and an offense against Jesus who laid down his life for us. God's desire for all of us is that we be holy as he is holy. I ask you to keep this at the forefront of your minds when you talk with those struggling with same-sex attractions. The victory is not in becoming heterosexual; it is in becoming holy. So Church, I hope my testimony lends a greater understanding and urgency to reach out in love and truth to your gay friends, neighbors, and family members.

"As for me, I no longer harbor bitterness or jealousy for being overlooked or unnoticed. I no longer am a slave to my sin nature, for he has set me free. My

Redeemer, my Savior, my Lord, my King, my everything is Jesus Christ. He loves me, and there is no greater love than his for me. The beautiful thing—the beauty from ashes—is that because I have been forgiven much that I love my Savior so much. In deliverance from my depraved life, he is glorified all the more.

"Finally, it is vital that we all understand that every struggle we face is part of spiritual warfare. It is real, and it is powerful. Homosexuality is a stronghold and a great delusion, and without God, we are doomed.

"I thank you for being here tonight, and I appreciate your prayers as I continue to share this testimony to as many people as will listen. Jesus' last words were a command to us 'to go into all the world and make disciples for Him.' I have been called to fulfill that command by making disciples of those who are still blinded by the distortions and lies of Satan about their true identity. Thank you for being here tonight, and may God bless you all.

Epilogue

Yahweh?

Yes, Gabriel.

Emory has glorified you, has she not?

Indeed, she has Gabriel, and all the more so through her great suffering. Her sifting has drawn her closer to me than she ever would have come otherwise. She has surely earned her crowns. When I call her home to me one day in her future, she will be among the ones who are most blessed, for she shall hear me say to her, 'Well done, my good and faithful servant.'

Amen and amen, Yahweh.

And, Gabriel, one more thing...

Yes, Lord?

It may well be that she shall see her Pepper again because I love all of my creation.

CPSIA information can be obtained
at www.ICGtesting.com
Printed in the USA
LVHW031314150821
695277LV00002B/8

9 781735 952970